Murder at Turtle Cove

by

Kathi Daley

This book is a work of fiction. Names, characters, places, and incidents either are products of the author's imagination or are used fictitiously. Any resemblance to actual events or locales or persons, living or dead, is entirely coincidental.

This book is dedicated to Linda Murray, a wonderful woman who maintained a positive attitude and inspired those around her in spite of her daily struggle with cancer. Linda, I want to take this opportunity to wish you one final good night.

I want to thank the very talented Jessica Fischer for the cover art.

I so appreciate Bruce Curran, who is always ready and willing to answer my cyber questions, and Peggy Hyndman for helping sleuth out those pesky typos.

And, of course, thanks to the readers and bloggers in my life, who make doing what I do possible.

Thank you to Randy Ladenheim-Gil for the editing.

Special thanks to Jeannie Daniel, Vivian Shane, Connie Correll, and Joanne Kocourek for submitting recipes.

And finally I want to thank my sister Christy for always lending an ear and my husband Ken for allowing me time to write by taking care of everything else.

Books by Kathi Daley

Come for the murder
Stay for the romance

Zoe Donovan Cozy Mystery:

Halloween Hijinks
The Trouble With Turkeys
Christmas Crazy
Cupid's Curse
Big Bunny Bump-off
Beach Blanket Barbie
Maui Madness
Derby Divas
Haunted Hamlet
Turkeys, Tuxes, and Tabbies
Christmas Cozy
Alaskan Alliance
Matrimony Meltdown
Soul Surrender
Heavenly Honeymoon
Hopscotch Homicide
Ghostly Graveyard
Santa Sleuth
Shamrock Shenanigans
Kitten Kaboodle
Costume Catastrophe

Candy Cane Caper
Holiday Hangover
Easter Escapade – *April 2017*

Zimmerman Academy The New Normal
Ashton Falls Cozy Cookbook

Tj Jensen Paradise Lake Mysteries by Henery Press

Pumpkins in Paradise
Snowmen in Paradise
Bikinis in Paradise
Christmas in Paradise
Puppies in Paradise
Halloween in Paradise
Treasure in Paradise – *April 2017*
Fireworks in Paradise – *October 2017*

Seacliff High Mystery:

The Secret
The Curse
The Relic
The Conspiracy
The Grudge

Whales and Tails Cozy Mystery:

Romeow and Juliet
The Mad Catter
Grimm's Furry Tail
Much Ado About Felines
Legend of Tabby Hollow
Cat of Christmas Past
A Tale of Two Tabbies
The Great Catsby
Count Catula
The Cat of Christmas Present
A Winter's Tail
The Taming of the Tabby – *June 2017*

Sand and Sea Hawaiian Mystery:

Murder at Dolphin Bay
Murder at Sunrise Beach
Murder at the Witching Hour
Murder at Christmas
Murder at Turtle Cove
Murder at Water's Edge – *May 2017*

Road to Christmas Romance:

Road to Christmas Past

Writer's Retreat Southern Mystery:

First Case – *May 2017*
Second Look – *July 2017*

Chapter 1

Tuesday, March 21

I sat on my surfboard, perfectly still, watching, waiting. The sun had just begun its ascent into the sky, creating a canvas of orange and red as it reflected off the clouds left from the overnight rain. I felt my body tense as I glanced toward the beach. Fins circled in a tight pattern coming increasingly closer to my dog, Sandy, who waited at the water's edge. I hoped and prayed Sandy would stay on the beach as he'd been trained to do. So far he'd been content to pace beyond the waterline, barking aggressively as the sharks enjoyed an early meal, but I suspected it was only a matter of time before he gave in to the urge to attack the intruders in order to remove the danger I was certain he could sense. My mind screamed *no* as he paced closer and closer to the waterline. I knew if I called out he would be more likely to attempt to swim out to me, so I just waited and prayed, then prayed and waited some more.

When I'd arrived that morning the beach and the water had been deserted, which wasn't all that unusual because the sun had yet to complete its climb over the horizon. Turtle Cove was isolated on the far northwestern corner of the island, known only to the locals who lived in the area. It wasn't likely to attract the casual surfer on holiday, which was why it was one of my favorite places to surf. I'd been enjoying some of the best waves I'd ever experienced in my life when I noticed the first of what would grow to be at least a half-dozen fins. Being a surfer living in the islands, I knew it was best to just hang back until the sharks had finished their meal, but hanging back and waiting had become an increasingly terrifying experience each time Sandy approached the water.

After several minutes the feeding frenzy came to an end and the sharks began to disperse. My heart beat just a bit faster as several of the sharks swam within arm's length of my surfboard on their way out of the cove. I lay flat on the fiberglass and tried not to move as two sharks approached the spot where I waited. They circled several times, inching closer with each pass, before moving on and continuing out to sea. It felt as if they could sense my presence and were curious but weren't sure what to make of me.

I had, on occasion, dove with the tiger sharks that populate the area. They're not only beautiful and graceful creatures but large predators, ranging from twelve to thirteen feet in length. Although tiger sharks can be dangerous and are responsible for attacks on swimmers and surfers each year, in Hawaii they're more than just ferocious predators. Here the shark, or *mano*, is woven into the fabric of Hawaiian culture and history. They're revered and even worshipped in many native traditions.

As soon as it looked as if the water was clear, I began to swim toward shore, quickly yet quietly. I paused between each stroke, listening for the return of my early morning friends. I scanned the water's surface as I tried to move silently through the sea. As I approached the beach, Sandy swam out and retrieved something floating on the surface. He dragged it back to the sand, and once I landed on the shore, he laid the prize at my feet. My hand flew to my mouth when I realized what it was he'd brought me. I gasped and turned away as I willed the nausea that had overtaken me to subside. I wasn't certain what I'd expected to find, but I certainly hadn't imagined Sandy's offering to be a *who* rather than a *what*. Or at least part of a who. I took several deep breaths, which seemed to quell my racing heart, before I ran to my bag, where I'd left my phone.

I called the Honolulu Police Department, then sat down on my towel and waited. The sun had peaked over the horizon and was climbing high into the sky. I knew it would be another perfect day in paradise, but somehow I couldn't quite find the focus to enjoy the day's awakening.

I bowed my head and tried to ignore the reality of what had just occurred. I knew these things happened. Shark attacks weren't common, but they certainly weren't unheard of. Still, as I glanced at the arm laying on the sand, I had a feeling something human rather than something from the sea had been behind this death. I wondered how it had ended up in the water, although I knew that wasn't my concern. The HPD was more than capable of taking care of things when they arrived. I just needed to wait for them. In the meantime I'd simply think happy thoughts.

The day had started off well enough. I'd woken early to find the surf outside the window of my oceanfront condo just about as perfect as it ever had been. I knew that if the surf there was raging, it must be off the charts just down the beach at Turtle Cove. I had a late start that day at my job as a WSO—water safety officer—for the Dolphin Bay Resort on the North Shore of Oahu, so I decided to grab Sandy and head down the coast to get in a few runs before I needed to be back to get ready for work.

The waves had been awesome, just as I'd predicted. I'd enjoyed several runs before the first of the fins appeared on the horizon. I hoped the shark was alone and would quickly be on its way, but within a few minutes a dozen of his friends had arrived to feed on something between where I was floating on the water and the beach.

I glanced at the waterproof sports watch I had spent a week's pay on so I would be less likely to lose track of time while riding the waves. There was no doubt about it; I was going to be late for work and I just knew that regardless of the reason for my late arrival, Drake Longboard, my immediate supervisor at the resort, was going to use my tardiness as a reason to stick me with the family pool. I supposed there wasn't much I could do about that at this point, so I put the matter out of my mind as I watched as a lone HPD vehicle pulled into the parking area. I stood up as Colin Reynolds, my brother Detective Jason Pope's partner, approached.

"Mornin', Lani," Colin greeted me. "I see you found another one."

"If an arm counts as a body then yeah, I guess I did."

Colin bent over and looked at the arm, which was really only part of one.

"Where's Jason?" I asked.

"I called him at home. He's on his way."

It was still early, so I should have realized Jason probably hadn't even been at work yet when I initially called. Jason is one of my five brothers, the second oldest and a detective for the HPD, married with two adorable children. Colin, who had been Jason's partner for a decade, lived close to the beach, whereas Jason and his family lived in a neighborhood located on the interior of the island, making his travel time to the crime scene that much further.

"I wonder who this belonged to," Colin mused.

I glanced at the arm, which was still laying on the sand, and felt my stomach begin to churn once again. "Blaze Whitmore," I answered.

"You know the guy?"

"Sort of. He's new to the island. He runs a food truck over on Aloha Beach."

"The burger-for-a-buck guy?"

"That would be him." I pointed to the tattoo on the forearm, which was incomplete because the upper arm was missing. "The partial tattoo you see was the lower half of a vine coiled around a cross."

"Seems like a vine wrapped around a cross is a fairly common tattoo."

"True, but this cross was different." I pointed to the arm. "See how the bottom is pointed? It almost looks like a knife. All four edges of the cross have that pointed shape and the cross was gray rather than brown or black."

"Was that it? Just a cross with a vine?"

I paused while I tried to picture the full tattoo. The cross had been drawn to appear cold and harsh, like the crossed steel of blades sans handles. The vine was thorny, with dark red accents that looked like blood. "No. There were words, or maybe it was just letters or even numbers, across the top." I remembered the letters, written in a bold yet fancy script that reminded me of roman numerals. "I can't remember what it said, but Blaze had become fairly well known in the short time he'd been on the island, so I'm sure someone—maybe Komo—can tell you." Komo Kamaka was a rival food truck vendor who had been born on the island and was known to pretty much everyone who had been around for any significant amount of time.

"I heard Komo and some of the others weren't real happy when this guy showed up and started selling his burgers for a buck."

"Can you blame them? Komo and the others had established a peaceful coexistence that worked for years. Each food truck had an agreed-upon territory and all the trucks kept their prices within a certain range. No one was getting rich, but they all made a living doing what they loved, and then this guy came on the scene a few months ago and started putting sandwich boards all over the North Shore offering a burger for a buck. Talk about upsetting the proverbial apple cart."

"I'm aware of the food truck war. I wonder if one of his rivals decided they'd had enough and killed him."

I glanced at the section of arm. Feeding a man to the sharks seemed an extreme way of dealing with competition, even if that competition had been in the process of destroying your way of life. "I know this guy was really hurting the bottom line for Komo and many of the others, but I don't think any of Blaze's rivals would kill him. How do you think he got in the water anyway?"

"Probably dumped from a boat within the past hour or two. The tide is strong this morning, which I would guess would account for him ending up here. Chances are the guy was either strangled or drowned. If there weren't any open wounds, the sharks might not have been attracted right away." Colin looked around. "My guess is, when the body washed into the cove the skin was torn on the sharp coral on the reef, alerting the sharks that breakfast was ready and waiting."

"I guess that makes sense. I'd been surfing for a good twenty minutes before the scavengers showed up."

I paused and looked toward the parking lot, where Jason had just pulled up. Like the rest of my brothers, he was a native Hawaiian of average height and build with dark hair, dark eyes, and brown skin. He wore his hair short and his uniform perfectly pressed.

"Lani," he greeted me as I watched him approach.

"Jason."

Jason turned to Colin. "What do we have?"

Colin filled him in.

Jason turned to me. "What time would you say you arrived?"

"I guess a little after six. Maybe as late as six-twenty. It was light enough to see what I was doing, but the sun hadn't risen yet."

"And how long were you here before the sharks arrived?"

"About twenty minutes. I have to work today, so I was planning to get in a few runs and then return home. I was waiting at the lineup when I noticed the first fin heading toward me."

"Was there anyone else in the water or on the beach?"

"No. Both the beach and the water were deserted except for Sandy."

Jason looked out over the sea toward the horizon. "The body can't have been in the water long. Did you notice any boats in the distance?"

"No. Do you think he was dumped this morning?"

"Probably within the past hour. I doubt we'll be able to identify an exact time of death, though, without the rest of the body."

Jason bent down to take a closer look at the arm. He pulled on a pair of latex gloves and turned it from side to side, studying both the intact hand and the tattoo on the forearm.

"I'm pretty sure it belonged to Blaze Whitmore," I provided.

"I thought I recognized the tat. I wish I could say I'm surprised to find the guy was most likely murdered, but based on everything that's been going on I figured it was only a matter of time before someone put some brawn behind their words."

"So you think one of the food truck vendors killed him?"

"Don't you? The guy has been stirring up a hornet's nest since he's been on the island."

I shrugged. "I don't know. I guess everyone was mad enough to want him gone, and I doubt his death will be mourned by many locally, but I'm having a hard time believing anyone from the food truck group would follow through with their threats and actually off the guy."

Jason stood up. He pulled off his gloves and once again looked out over the horizon. "Maybe it wasn't one of the truck owners. I've spoken to the man on several occasions and he had a way about him that made you want to punch him. While the competition angle is one I plan to investigate, I plan to look into the other areas of his life. Do you happen to know if he was married?"

"I'm not sure. I didn't have a lot of direct contact with him. He seemed to have a lot of money; more than you'd expect a food truck vendor to have. I guess he might have brought money with him when he came to the island. Oh, and I remember Komo saying Blaze was new to the industry. I think he mentioned he was some sort of businessman before moving to Oahu." I looked toward the parking lot. Several cars had pulled up while we chatted. "It looks like we have company."

"I'll send them on their way and put up a barrier at the entrance of the lot," Colin offered.

Jason turned and looked toward the parking area. "Yeah, that's a good idea. You may as well put out a sign letting folks know the beach will be closed for the day. I have divers on the way. If there are any other remains we need to find them before the tide shifts. My theory is the body was dumped from a boat, but I'm going to have the crime scene guys search the sand just in case there's something there."

"And the arm?" I asked.

"We'll bag it and take it in for the medical examiner to look at once the crime scene guys give us the all clear to remove whatever we find of the victim."

"I'm not sure I can tell you much more than I already have and I'm already late for work, so I was hoping you'd let me go. Drake has been particularly difficult to work with lately and I don't want to give him any more reason than he already has to ruin my life. If you have additional questions or need me to do anything, you know where to find me."

"That's fine. I'll call you later."

Chapter 2

"Kill me now," I said to no one in particular as I sat on the lifeguard stand at the family pool.

I work with five other WSOs who all rotate between the surfing beach, the family beach, and, the worst assignment of all, the family pool. Our actual boss, Mitch Hamilton, knows that I absolutely loathe the family pool, so back when he was the one doling out the assignments, he would more often than not spare me the pain. Then, a little less than a year ago, he'd promoted Drake, my archrival, to the position of his assistant and turned the scheduling over to him.

"No running," I yelled at a group of kids ranging in age from post-toddler to preteen who insisted on running around the exterior of the pool no matter how many times I warned them not to. I'm generally a nice person who can get along with a variety of people, but with the exception of my niece and nephew, who I adore, kids and I generally mix about as well as oil and water.

"Excuse me, miss, but my daughter needs to go to the bathroom and I just smeared oil all over my body. If I move around too much it gets in my hair. Do you think you could take her?"

I looked at the sunburned haole dressed in the tiniest bikini I'd ever seen and explained that my title was WSO, not babysitter.

God, I hated the family pool.

If I made it through this shift with my sanity intact I was going to have a chat with my snake of a supervisor and somehow talk him into reassigning me for the following day. While this might be considered a reasonable request in some circles, the truth of the matter was that Drake and I had never gotten along. It pretty much had been hate at first sight when we met and our opinion of each other hadn't softened with time. If Drake could make my life miserable without making himself look bad, you could count on that being exactly what he'd do.

There are days when I'd decide I really needed to quit this job and move on, but then someone would remind me that I make good money doing something I loved most of the time and putting up with Drake was really a small price to pay to keep me out of the fast-food industry.

"Lady," a boy who looked to be seven or eight said from the foot of my chair.

"Yes?"

"I had an accident."

"An accident?"

He turned and looked toward the pool, where the evidence of his accident was clearly visible.

This day just kept getting better and better.

"Okay; thanks for letting me know." I picked up my megaphone. "Everyone out of the pool. I'm sorry for the inconvenience, but we'll need to temporarily close the pool for decontamination."

Apparently everyone knew what that meant because everyone scrambled out as quickly as if I'd just announced the water had turned to acid.

"Lani to base," I said into my handheld radio.

"Go for Drake."

"Accident in the pool."

"Did you evacuate?"

"I just did."

"Then let me know when you have it cleaned up."

"Me?" I screeched. "Don't we have maintenance people for that?"

"Doug is alone today and he went to lunch. You know what to do, so get to it. Call me when you're done."

Have I mentioned I hate the family pool?

As I cleaned and decontaminated the pool, I let my mind drift to the arm Sandy had found that morning. I wondered if the divers had been able to recover any more of the body or if the sharks had been thorough diners. As much as I hated the idea that Komo or one of the other food truck owners might have gone to such extreme measures to eliminate the man they'd all grown to loathe, the more I thought about it, that was exactly the sort of thing one or more of them might have been motivated enough to do.

Not that they were a violent group. Just the opposite, in fact. But there was a unique tradition surrounding the food trucks that populated the island and the culture, custom, and way of life the industry provided meant a lot more to the men and women who worked the trucks than just the income they derived from them. When Blaze Whitmore came along with his fancy truck and loss-leader pricing, he not only threatened the ability of his competitors to make a living but he threatened the culture as well.

I glanced at my watch and quickly calculated how long it would take for the chemicals I'd added to the pool to do their thing once I'd removed the solid matter. It would be another hour at least, so I decided to take my break then. I pulled on a pair of shorts and a T-shirt over my bathing suit and headed indoors. Once I entered the air-conditioned main building, I crossed the lobby toward the reservation desk where my best friend, cousin, and roommate Kekoa Pope was working that day.

"Heard the family pool is closed," Kekoa, who had long black hair, brown eyes, and brown skin, greeted me from behind the counter. She was dressed in a crisp white blouse and black skirt, which made her look pulled together and professional.

"A torpedo."

Kekoa scrunched up her nose. "Ew."

"Tell me about it. I thought this day started off on a pretty disgusting note, but it seems it just keeps getting grosser and grosser."

"I also heard about your little adventure this morning. Have you heard from Jason?"

"No. I'll call him later if he doesn't get back to me. Did you also hear the victim was most likely the new food truck guy?"

She nodded. "Most likely? Was there any doubt?"

I grabbed the rubber band from my shorts pocket and pulled my hair into a sloppy bun. "The partial arm Sandy discovered had the bottom half of a tattoo on it. I'm sure it'll turn out to belong to Blaze Whitmore, but they'll have to pull a print off the hand, which was intact, to know for sure. I can't help wondering if one of the rival food truck owners was responsible for the early morning feeding frenzy."

"You don't think Komo...?"

"No. Not Komo specifically, although he did threaten to take matters into his own hands if HPD didn't do something about the guy poaching his customers."

"Yeah, but Komo is a sweetie and he must have realized that while Blaze was a snake, he wasn't doing anything illegal."

I jumped up and sat down on the counter. Then I reached over and snagged a piece of gum from the drawer where I knew Kekoa kept her stash. "I think that's the real problem. If Whitmore was doing something illegal HPD could have shut him down. Short of a legal reason to make him gone, a violent reason might have seemed necessary. The guy was creating a real problem. Once the food trucks began to lose business to the burger-for-a-buck deal, the business that was left became a valuable commodity and the competition between the vendors, who had previously existed harmoniously, began to intensify to the point where there's been all sorts of feuding."

"The guy had only been on the island for a few months," Kekoa pointed out.

"Exactly. And look at the damage he did in that short time. I heard Zipper and Sarge got into a fistfight the other day. They used to be the best of friends." The two men were vendors who specialized in burgers and sandwiches much like the ones being served at the burger-for-a-buck truck.

"I guess I never stopped to consider the fallout from having a delicate balance totally destroyed." Kekoa paused to answer the phone before she continued. "Do you think Zipper or Sarge could commit murder?"

I shrugged. "I don't know. Maybe. Zipper is a really intense guy, and I know he spent time in prison before moving to the island and setting up his food truck. And Sarge is ex-military. You can tell just by speaking to him that he has demons he barely manages to keep at bay. I suppose if Blaze did or said something to set one of them off, ending up as shark bait might very well be the result."

I checked my phone while Kekoa handed a list of repairs to the guest services worker who'd stopped by to pick it up. There were two texts. One was from my oldest brother, who lived on Maui and worked for Maui PD, telling me to call my mother, and the other was from my mother, complaining that I hadn't been by to visit in over a week. I loved my mother, I really did, but she seemed to be suffering from some sort of intensified empty nest syndrome ever since my youngest brother got married. Mom and my new sister-in-law didn't get along, so my brother's frequent visits to my parents' house had come to an abrupt halt, leaving Mom at loose ends. What she really needed was a hobby. I thought that once my dad retired the pair would travel, or at least keep each other occupied, but he seemed to have his friends and his interests and she stayed home day after day, as she had for much of her life.

"Are we all set for tonight?" I asked after Kekoa returned her attention to our conversation. Kekoa and I lived in a condominium complex with five other units. Today was the birthday of our next-door neighbor, Elva Talbot, and Kekoa and I had planned a party for her at my boyfriend's place. We'd invited the other residents of the complex, as well as a few of Elva's friends from the senior center.

"We are," Kekoa said. "I told everyone to be at Luke's at around six. I thought we'd just BBQ on the patio. Everyone from the complex has confirmed, as have the five people from the senior center. I was just planning on doing steaks and sides. You aren't aware of any food restrictions of the seniors, are you?"

"As far as I know, none of them have any restrictions. Janice usually stays away from dairy, but I think that's by choice, not a medical issue. Tammy Rhea is almost always on a diet, but I don't think there's anything she *can't* eat, and Beth is a vegetarian and usually brings along her own rabbit food when we have dinner parties."

"I have a green salad as well as veggie kabobs and sourdough bread if she doesn't bring her own food."

"Are you going to make potato mac?"

Kekoa tucked her long black hair behind one ear. "I already did. It's in the refrigerator, so as long as Cam doesn't eat it before I get off work we should be good to go."

"Did you remind Cam to pick up the cake at the bakery?"

"I did and he said he would."

Cameron Carrington is Kekoa's boyfriend and our third roommate. Cam and I had been friends since we were teens, and we both applied for jobs at the resort after we graduated high school. We found the condo complex, which is close to the resort as well as right on the beach, and Cam and I leased a two-bedroom apartment to share the rent. I invited Kekoa to live with us and she and I share a room; having a third roommate was really the only way we could afford a place in such a prime location.

Kekoa paused to answer the phone. When she finished the call she asked if I had spoken to Shredder recently: another of the residents in the complex. I hadn't and asked why she'd asked.

"You know how Shredder is Mr. Mystery Guy?"

"Yeah, I know," I answered. "What about it?" Shredder was nice enough, but he never shared any personal information with any of us. It was as if the door connecting his present to his past was firmly closed, with a big "Stay Out" sign on it. There'd been a time when his fierce secrecy had really bothered me, but after he'd saved my life on the ocean last summer, I'd decided he was entitled to keep his past to himself and began to accept him as he was, without worrying about who he was or what he might have done before I met him.

"I saw him this morning. Here, at the resort. I thought it was odd, so I followed him, and you'll never guess where he went."

"Where?" Dolphin Bay wasn't the sort of place where Shredder normally hung out, but I still didn't see why his coming here would cause Kekoa to go all James Bond in the middle of her shift.

"Remember the guy I told you about yesterday?"

"The guy who checked in a few days ago wearing a black suit, black dress shoes, and dark glasses who you were sure was FBI or CIA?"

"Yes, the man in bungalow six."

"That's who Shredder was visiting?"

"Yep. So do you still think I was imagining things when I told you I thought the guy was a fed? I bet the guy is

Shredder's handler. Or maybe he's here to investigate Shredder. Or even arrest him."

"If Shredder is on the run and the guy was here to arrest him, Shredder wouldn't willingly go visit him."

"That's true. Maybe Shredder is a spy."

"Shredder never goes anywhere. Spies travel a lot. But he might be in witness protection. Or maybe he's some sort of an informant. Do you know anything else about the guy in bungalow six?"

"I know his name is Vince Kensington and he paid cash for a two-week stay. I mean, who pays cash for anything anymore?"

"Yeah, I guess that is odd, but that doesn't necessarily make him a fed."

"He's passed by the desk several times, and every time he's wearing that same black suit, or at least a similar one, and I'm pretty sure he has a gun because I noticed a bulge under his jacket. If he comes by again I'm going to drop something to see if I can get him to bend over. His jacket wasn't buttoned, so it should hang open and I can get a look at what he's hiding underneath."

I grinned at Kekoa. "It looks like I'm rubbing off on you."

Kekoa sighed. "I'm afraid you might be right. At least I haven't broken into his bungalow to try to find out what he's up to, which is the sort of thing you would do."

"It does seem like our next move."

"He most likely has a gun," Kekoa reminded me.

"Do you want to know what his deal is or not?"

"I'm curious," Kekoa admitted, "but I'm not sure I'm curious enough to actually break into his room."

"Maybe you aren't curious enough, but I am. I wonder if he's in there right now."

Kekoa didn't know.

"Call his room," I suggested. "If he answers ask him if he needs anything. If he doesn't I'll check it out."

"The man has a gun," Kekoa reminded me once again.

"Which is inconsequential if he isn't in his room. Call."

Kekoa did as I asked. Mr. Kensington didn't answer, so I grabbed the master key, picked up a stack of towels from one of the maids' carts, and headed to bungalow six. I figured I'd knock on the door to be sure he wasn't there. If he answered I'd tell him I was there to deliver the extra towels he'd requested. If he denied asking for the towels I'd apologize and tell him I must have written down the wrong room. Of course he might find it odd that a WSO would be delivering towels, but if he asked I could say I was on a break and had been asked to drop them off on my way to lunch.

I passed the family beach and continued down the walkway, lined with colorful hibiscus, then passed the fork that led to the beach bar and continued to the bungalows. I knocked on the door of bungalow six. There was no answer. I knocked again and called out "Housekeeping" as I entered the room. I set the towels on the bathroom counter and headed back to the seating area at the front of the bungalow. There was a computer set up on the table near the window, but otherwise the room held few personal possessions. I headed to the bedroom and paused to take a look around. The bed was unmade, which led me to suspect the maid hadn't been by yet. I opened the closet and found five black suits, all identical, along with at least a half dozen white shirts. Who comes to Hawaii and wears nothing but dark suits?

I looked down and noticed several pairs of shoes on the floor of the closet, all black, alongside a briefcase that, I quickly realized, was locked.

I closed the closet doors and looked around the room. There was a blank pad of paper on the bedside table with a blue pen next to it with the cap off. Perhaps he'd made a note and then taken it with him. I pulled off the next sheet of paper on the top of the pad in case it held an impression of whatever might have been written on top of it. If the man *was* CIA or FBI chances were he'd be smart enough not to leave that sort of information behind, but it didn't hurt to check it out.

I was about to start opening drawers when I heard someone at the door. I quickly dropped to the floor and then scrambled under the bed. I could only see the floor in front of me from my vantage point, but that was enough for me to identify the arrival as a maid. I knew I would have a hard time explaining why I was under the bed, so I waited for her to make the bed and move onto the bathroom. I should be able to sneak out of the bungalow while she scrubbed the shower.

"What are you doing in here?" I heard a deep voice ask.

"My name is Marta. I'm with housekeeping. I'm here to make up the bed and straighten the room. I can come back later to finish if this isn't a good time."

"The bed is fine. I already told the other woman I didn't require cleaning services."

"I'm so sorry, sir. This is my first day back after my vacation and no one passed on your request to me. Can I get you anything at all?"

"I noticed a stack of fresh towels in the bathroom, so I should be fine. I'll call the desk if I need anything else."

"Very well, sir. Enjoy your stay."

Wonderful. Now I was trapped under the bed until the man who, according to Kekoa, never went anywhere, decided to go somewhere.

I was considering my options when his phone rang.

"Yeah?"

He paused, I imagined to listen to the person on the other end of the line.

"I stumbled onto a new lead, so I'm going to stay to check it out."

He paused for another minute before saying he'd be in contact in a few days and then hung up.

Maybe he really was FBI or CIA. Or a spy of some other sort. I hadn't seen anything more than his feet so far, but even the shoes he wore screamed espionage.

The man turned and headed toward the bathroom. I realized this was my chance to make my escape, so I crawled out from under the bed and quietly made my way to the front of the bungalow. I had just opened the door when I heard the water in the sink turn off. I quickly scrambled out, closing the door just a bit too loudly behind me. I hid behind some shrubs seconds before he opened the front door to look around. I could swear he looked right at me, but he didn't approach, so perhaps he hadn't seen me after all.

I waited a few minutes before leaving my hiding spot behind the shrubs. Then I hurried back to the lobby, where I'd left my staff radio. Drake would be expecting me to check in with him about the status of the pool and if I had any chance of being assigned a different post the following day I needed to avoid making him angry.

"So?" Kekoa asked as I handed her the key and retrieved the radio.

"I think you're right about the guy. I'm not sure if he's a good guy or a bad one, but he definitely seems to have business on the island, and while I hate to admit it, I suspect, based on the timing of

Shredder's visit, it has something to do with him. Do you have a pencil?"

Kekoa handed me a recently sharpened yellow #2. I carefully scribbled the lead over the surface of the paper I'd taken from the bungalow to see if I could pick up a clue from it. There was a word, although it was faint. I could only make out parts of the letters, but it appeared to say *park*. Was Kensington meeting someone in the park? Or maybe he was meeting someone named Park or even Parker? Or had he written *parking garage* and the second word hadn't come through?

"There's not enough here to tell us anything. I know you said Kensington was staying close to his bungalow, but have you noticed him leave or has anyone else visited him?"

"I haven't seen him leave, but then, he wouldn't necessarily have come through the lobby if he had, and as far as I know he hasn't had any other visitors, although again, there's no way I'd know if he did. The only reason I knew Shredder had visited was because I know him and I know Dolphin Bay isn't a place he frequents, so when he walked by on the path outside the window, I was curious and followed him."

Kekoa had a point. There were a lot of people coming and going here at all hours of the day. Unless something or someone stood out as odd chances were no one would notice.

"How about the phone?" I asked. "Has anyone called him on the resort phone?"

"Not that I know of. Kensington has a cell; most people do. The room phones are rarely used other than to call for room service, make a reservation at one of the restaurants, or schedule spa treatments."

Kensington didn't seem the sort to go in for spa treatments, but maybe he'd ordered from room service or made a dinner reservation. "Can you see if he's made any of those calls?"

Kekoa hesitated. "Would it really tell you anything if he had?"

"Probably not, but aren't you curious anyway?"

Kekoa sighed, but she did turn to her computer and begin to type in a series of commands. "You realize that one of these days your curiosity is going to get me fired?"

"All you're doing is looking up guest reservations. I doubt you're going to get fired even if someone figures out what you're doing."

"I hope you're right. The last thing I need is to have to look for another job." Kekoa looked at the screen in front of her. "It looks like Mr. Kensington has a reservation in the steak house for eight o'clock this evening."

"How many people is the reservation for?"

"Two."

"Reserve me a table for two at eight."

"What about Elva's party?"

"The party is at five. The seniors aren't likely to linger once the food is served, so I'm sure the party will be over before eight."

"Maybe, but we're BBQing. It will seem odd if you don't have anything, so if you go to the steak house at eight you're going to have to eat two dinners."

"I won't eat much at the party. No one will notice if I just nibble. I'll tell Luke not to eat much as well. Maybe if we see who Kensington is meeting we can find out what he's up to."

"He might not be up to anything other than a tropical vacation," Kekoa reminded me.

"Maybe not, but my gut tells me he is, and if that something involves Shredder I want to know what it is."

Kekoa shook her head. "It never ceases to amaze me how willing you are to totally disrupt your life simply to appease your curiosity."

"Hey, you're the one who started this whole thing by telling me that Shredder had visited the guy. What if Shredder is in some sort of trouble?" I glanced at the clock. "I should get back before Drake realizes I'm AWOL. I'll see you at the party."

Chapter 3

"Happy birthday to you, happy birthday to you, happy birthday dear Elva, happy birthday to you," everyone sang.

Elva, who was dressed in a pretty pink and white muumuu with large flowers on the front, was positively beaming. She wasn't only our next-door neighbor but a sweet woman Kekoa and I adored. I'd only known her a few years, but from what I could tell she didn't have any family. Based on the happy glow that had pinkened her cheeks, she hadn't been on the receiving end of a birthday celebration for a very long time.

"Thank you, everyone," Elva said with tears on her cheeks. "I can't tell you how much this means to me."

"Open your presents," Tammy Rhea ordered. "The big one with the orange paper is from Emmy Jean and me."

Tammy Rhea recently had moved to the island to be near her sister, Emmy Jean Thornton, although she'd been well known to the group because she'd visited the island frequently before that. Tammy Rhea and Emmy Jean were flamboyant Southern ladies who were part of the senior sleuthing gang that had helped Luke and me track down two killers in the past year. I knew if the subject of the arm on the beach came up the sisters would jump onto a boat I had no intention of sailing, so I'd counseled both Cam and Kekoa not to mention it at the party.

"A wig?" Elva asked as she lifted the bright pink aberration from the box.

"It's to go with the makeover me and Emmy Jean are going to give you," Tammy Rhea explained.

Elva glanced at me and I shrugged. Tammy Rhea was sporting purple hair today. In the year I'd known her, she'd changed her hair color five times. Tammy Rhea was a well-endowed woman who liked to play up her assets by creating outrageous looks that ensured she'd never get lost in a crowd.

"Thank you for the thought, but I'm not sure pink hair will work on me," Elva responded.

"Which is why Emmy Jean suggested the wig instead of permanent color. If you don't like how you look after we have our spa day you can wash off the makeup and take off the wig."

Kekoa picked up a gift card from the bottom of the box. "It says here that in addition to a makeover the day includes a massage and a pedicure. That'll be nice, don't you think?"

Elva looked more horrified than happy, but she agreed that a pedicure might be nice.

"Open mine next," ten-year-old Malia said persuasively. Malia was a petite native Hawaiian who had moved to the complex with her Aunt Mary after the death of her mother. Elva, who had lost her only child many years ago, had bonded with the girl, taking on the role of honorary grandmother.

I watched as Elva opened the box holding a small throw Malia had knitted with Mary's help. I could see the handcrafted item meant a lot to her. The throw was followed by a Fitbit from uberhealthy senior Beth Wasserman and a very pretty silk scarf from condo residents Kevin Green and Sean Trainor. Carina West, a hula dancer who had specifically requested a night off to attend the party, gave Elva a vase that had been handmade by one of the locals who worked the craft fairs on the island. Several of Elva's other friends gave her gift cards for local restaurants she favored.

By the time she'd worked through the entire pile of gifts several of the guests were gathering their belongings in preparation for heading home. I looked at my watch. It was only six-forty. There would be plenty of time for Luke and me to change and make it to the resort by eight.

"Now that Elva has opened her gifts I have an announcement to make," Janice Furlong, the oldest of the senior women in attendance announced. Everyone stopped what they were doing. "RJ and I are getting married."

RJ Clark was a fifty-five-year-old local newscaster who'd only recently begun dating seventy-five-year-old Janice.

"Married?" Beth asked.

I had to hand it to Janice. She'd decided at the ripe old age of seventy-five that she wanted to get married again and it looked as if she'd managed to do what she'd set out to do.

"A week from Saturday. RJ has a busy work schedule and at my age I don't want to wait, so we're going to elope, but I wanted you all to know."

"But you can't elope," Emmy Jean, whose platinum-blond hair was teased so that it stood high on her head, insisted. "We all want to be there. We want to throw you a party. It's the proper thing to do."

"RJ doesn't want a fuss."

"We don't need to fuss," Emmy Jean said. "We can have something right here at the ranch, with just a few friends in attendance."

Janice glanced at Luke.

"I'd be happy to have it here if that's what you and RJ decide to do."

"Then it's settled," Emmy Jean announced, clapping her hands together in such a way that her long purple fingernails reflected the overhead light. "What time are we meeting tomorrow?"

"Tomorrow?" I asked.

"We need to start planning. Say around noon?"

"I'm meeting with a man who's interested in one of my horses tomorrow afternoon," Luke informed her. "I probably won't be home until five or even five-thirty."

"And I have work until four-thirty," I added.

"Then dinner it is," Emmy Jean said. "We'll meet here at six. If Luke will provide the meat the girls and I will bring the sides."

I glanced helplessly at Luke while the senior women firmed up plans for the following day. It wasn't that I didn't enjoy spending time with them, but any time they could fabricate an excuse to spend time at Luke's ranch they did so. Luke was a good guy who had pointed out on more than one occasion that he was happy to be able to bring a little adventure into the women's lives, but there were times I found myself wishing he and I had a bit more time to ourselves.

Kekoa giggled. "I think the senior sleuthing brigade has you and Luke wrapped around their little fingers."

"Tell me about it. At least all they have planned is a party and not sleuthing this time."

"Speaking of sleuthing, you haven't heard from Shredder, have you? I thought he'd be here."

I frowned. I had to admit his absence from the party had bothered me. Shredder was quiet, but he seemed to enjoy socializing with the condo crowd. "No. I stopped by his place before I came out to the ranch, but it was dark. Wherever he went he took Riptide," I said, referring to Shredder's dog.

"Then everything must be okay," Kekoa concluded.

"I guess." I actually wasn't so sure. I was about to say as much when my phone beeped to let me know I had a new text. It was from Jason, saying the arm I'd found had been confirmed to have belonged to Blaze Whitmore.

"Is there a problem?" Kekoa asked.

I glanced up from the phone. "No. There isn't a problem." I quickly explained what had been in Jason's text.

"Arm? What arm?" Emmy Jean said from behind me.

Dang. I'd been hoping to get through the party without bringing the seniors into what I was certain would turn out to be a messy murder investigation.

"It's nothing," I tried.

"I heard you say that your brother confirmed the arm belonged to Blaze Whitmore," Emmy Jean insisted. She turned and looked at the crowd. "Did you hear that? Lani found an arm!"

Of course once that announcement was made I was forced to give an abbreviated accounting of the day's events. Luckily, I was able to keep the questions to a minimum and send the ladies on their way in time for Luke and me to make our reservation.

******

The steak house at the Dolphin Bay was considered one of the nicest on the island, but this was still Hawaii, so dress tended toward dressy casual rather than formal. Luke had changed into a dress shirt and dark slacks and I had decided on a short red halter dress paired with one of the few pairs of heels I owned. I didn't have a lot of time to fuss with my hair, so I pulled it back on one side before applying a light coat of mascara and some rose-colored lip gloss.

"Seems like the party went well," Luke commented as we drove to the resort.

"Elva really seemed happy. I'm so glad Kekoa thought to arrange it."

"The food looked wonderful. Too bad we couldn't eat much of it."

I was sure I'd heard Luke's stomach growl. Not that my own hadn't been complaining as well. "The food at the steak house is really good," I assured him. "I'm betting you'll be glad you didn't fill up at the party. If you take the next left you can park around back. It's an employee lot, but it's closer to the steak house than the public one and I have a feeling I'm not going to want to walk far in these shoes."

Luke turned where I indicated.

"Don't take this the wrong way," he began. "You look absolutely beautiful and very sexy, but I'm sort of surprised you wore heels. I've heard you liken them to a torture device."

"I do. Usually. I bought these shoes on a whim in Honolulu a few years ago and rarely have reason to wear them. When I realized we were going to be dining in the steak house I figured what the heck. Of course my feet are already killing me, so you may have to carry me back to the truck at the end of the night."

Luke grinned. "I'd be happy to."

Luckily, he found a parking spot near the front of the lot so the walk to the steak house was a relatively short one. It was a warm night, with only a gentle breeze. I could hear the sound of the waves in the distance as we traveled the well-lit walkway that curved throughout the whole resort. I leaned my head on Luke's shoulder as we made our way to the entrance of the oceanfront restaurant. He and I spent a lot of time together and ate out frequently, but we'd settled into a comfortable routine in which we rarely had an actual date night.

"I almost didn't recognize you," the host, who I was certain had never seen me in anything other than a bathing suit or shorts and a tee, commented. "Do you have a reservation?"

"We do. It looks like you're busy."

"Packed. It's Saturday night."

I looked around the crowded waiting area. "So I assume requesting a specific table is out of the question?"

"You assume right. We already have all the tables set up for the reservations we have. I see you're at table seven."

"Is a man named Vince Kensington dining here this evening?"

"Yes. He's already seated at table twenty-eight."

I didn't know for certain, but it didn't sound like tables seven and twenty-eight were anywhere near each other. How was I supposed to spy on the man if he was seating on the other side of a crowded room? "I don't suppose you have a two-top closer to table twenty-eight that we can trade for?"

The host gave me an odd look, which I supposed I understood given the situation. "Are the two of you together?"

"No. Not at all. Never mind. Can I take a look at the table you have reserved for us before we're seated?"

"Certainly, if you'd like."

I stepped around the desk used by the host and cashier and entered the restaurant. I tried to find Kensington in the crowd. I'd only had a brief glimpse of him when he'd looked out the door of his bungalow while I hid in the bushes, but I was pretty sure he was the man who was sitting alone near the window. If Luke and I took the table to which we'd been assigned we would be too far away to hear anything that was said there, so I thought we might as well bag the idea and try to figure out what Kensington was up to another way.

"Maybe we'll wait and come back when you're less crowded," I said to the host.

"We have people waiting, so whatever you decide is fine with me."

I looked at Luke. "Should we just grab something at the beach bar?"

"That sounds good to me. I'm starving, so quicker is better."

I turned back to the host. "It's fine to give the table away."

"Very well." He looked at his list and called the next twosome to the front.

I pulled Luke aside. "Based on the seating chart, Kensington is the man sitting alone near the last window before the hallway leading to the restrooms. I'm going to go pay a quick visit to the ladies' room so I can at least snap a photo of him. Why don't you head over to the beach bar and grab us a table? It's likely to be crowded as well. I'll meet you there in a few minutes."

"Okay, but be careful. If the guy is a fed, as Kekoa thinks, he'll have been trained to be aware of his surroundings. He may not appreciate having his photo taken."

"I'll be careful."

Luke left the restaurant while I headed toward the restroom. I'd decided it would be easiest to walk past Kensington, then take the photo from the hallway, so I made an effort to look directly in front of me as I passed his table. I planned to go into the restroom in case he happened to have been watching me. I waited a couple of minutes and then reentered the hallway, pausing when I saw a second man had joined Kensington. This man's back was to me, but based on the long, bleached blond hair, I was pretty sure Kensington's dinner companion was Shredder. That would explain why he hadn't been at Elva's party.

I plastered myself against the wall and took a photo. I was too far away to hear what they were saying, but I didn't dare move closer. If the man with his back to me was Shredder, he'd recognize me, which was something I wasn't sure I wanted to happen. I didn't know what Shredder was mixed up in, which meant I wasn't sure whether he was meeting with a good guy or a bad one. Given what I suspected had been Blaze Whitmore's recent fate, I wasn't certain I wanted to draw attention to my snooping activities.

Kensington said something to the man I thought was Shredder that made him turn around and look in my direction. I flattened myself against the wall, then scooted back to the restroom. I thought I'd managed to make it inside without being seen, but now I was trapped. If I walked out the way I'd come in Shredder would see me, and now I was snooping for sure.

I paused to consider my options but eventually decided that despite my very tight, very short dress, my almost nonexistent thong underwear, and my high heels, I was going to have to climb up on the sink and slip out the window. I suddenly wished I'd opted for cotton briefs and a dress that was more spy worthy and hoped I'd be able to make my escape with at least a small piece of my dignity intact.

Unfortunately, a group of women came into the ladies' room just as I was sprawled in my most compromising position, with one leg out the window and the other still balanced on the sink.

Once I completed my escape I took off my heels and carried them in my hand as I headed to the beach bar.

"Kensington's guest showed up. I'm pretty sure it was Shredder," I said to Luke upon arriving at the table he'd managed to procure.

"Shredder? The steak house doesn't seem like his sort of place."

"I agree, but I'm pretty sure it was him." I pulled up the photo on my camera and showed it to Luke, who narrowed his eyes as he studied it. It wasn't a lot to go on, but Shredder wore his hair quite a bit longer than the current trend.

"It only shows the back of his head and shoulders, although based on the hair and build it could definitely be Shredder," Luke commented. "Didn't you get a look at his face when you left the restaurant?"

"I didn't leave through the front. When I realized the second man might be Shredder I panicked and went out the bathroom window."

"Why?"

"I didn't want him to know I was spying on him."

"Why would he think that? Even if he saw you, wouldn't he assume you were in the restaurant for dinner?"

I paused. "Yeah. I guess I really didn't think things through. I'm pretty sure Kensington saw me watching them. He said something to his companion, who started to turn around, so I scooted down the hallway to the bathroom. I don't think his guest saw me. Let's get out of here. Suddenly I feel the need to regroup."

"Maybe you should just ask Shredder what's going on. If his business with Kensington is as supersecret as you seem to think it is, they most likely wouldn't be meeting in a restaurant."

"That's true. I suppose I might be seeing espionage where none exists. Maybe Shredder will be home tomorrow and I can have a chat with him. It would be nice to put this mystery at least to bed. I'm sorry I wasted your time."

"You didn't waste my time, but I do think you might be making a bigger deal out of Shredder knowing this guy than makes sense. Even if the guy is a fed, as Kekoa thinks, that doesn't mean Shredder is related to him in any sort of official way.

For all we know, the man could be Shredder's uncle or an old family friend."

"Maybe, but my gut is telling me otherwise. Let's get out of here anyway. I can't wait to get out of this dress."

"Now that," Luke grinned, "is something I'm more than happy to assist you with."

Chapter 4

I woke in the middle of the night to see a light outside the window. I glanced over at Luke, who was snoring softly, before climbing out of bed. I slipped on the pair of shorts, T-shirt, and sweatshirt I'd discarded on a nearby chair before dressing for the steak house. Then I slipped my feet into a pair of flip-flops and stepped over the dogs, who we'd taken swimming before turning in for the night. They were all so exhausted I didn't think an earthquake would wake them.

I grabbed a flashlight from the kitchen, although I didn't turn it on. I headed out the side door and paused. It was a clear night and the moon was high in the sky, providing adequate light. I stood perfectly still and listened once I'd made my way onto the drive, away from the pool. I could hear the waves in the distance, but little other sound pierced the darkness. Based on the position of the bedroom window, I had to assume the light had come from the north pasture. I looked in that direction, but I didn't see a light or any sign of an intruder. Luke and the dogs were safe inside, so my primary concern was for the horses on the property. Luke had taken them into the barn for the night, so I headed there.

Luke's ranch was fairly isolated, so it wasn't as if people cut through it as a means of getting from one place to another. There were, however, quite a few homeless people on the island, and I'd recently noticed a camp had been set up not far from here. I didn't necessarily think a member of the homeless population would hurt the horses even if that was who I'd seen, but it was a warm, dry night, so it seemed unlikely that our visitor was someone simply seeking shelter.

I quietly opened the barn door so as not to alert a possible intruder to my presence. I didn't see a light or hear anything that would indicate there was anyone in the building. I stepped into the darkness and looked around. The barn smelled of fresh hay and manure, and the only sounds I heard were the soft snorts of the horses, most likely curious about who had disturbed them at this time of the night. I turned around and was going to head back to the house when I heard a sneeze.

"Who's there?" I demanded as I clicked on my flashlight.

No one answered, but I did hear a scurrying in the stall where Luke's newest foal was kept. I took several steps in that direction, my heart beating with each movement. I couldn't see anyone in the stall, so I scooted up to the side and looked over the wooden door.

"Well, I'll be. What are you doing in here?"

The child, who I assumed was seven or eight judging by his size, glared at me with fearful eyes.

"I'm not going to hurt you," I assured him. "What's your name?"

"T-t-tommy."

"Well, Tommy, why don't you come on out of there so we can have a chat?"

"Are you going to call the police?" The boy, who obviously hadn't had a bath in days, looked like he would flee at a moment's notice if I answered incorrectly.

"No, I'm not going to call the police. I just want to talk to you. Are you hungry?"

Tommy's eyes grew at least two sizes.

"I can make you a sandwich if you want."

He stood up slowly. It was at that point I noticed the kitten he had clutched to his chest. "Is that your kitten?" I asked.

"He lives under the barn. There are three of them. I think the mom left, so I like to check on them when I can."

Luke hadn't mentioned kittens. Maybe he didn't know. There were a lot of feral cats on the island, so kittens seemed to pop up everywhere.

"Maybe the kitten would like some milk. Why don't you bring it inside?"

The boy, who was dressed in filthy shorts and a faded T-shirt, nodded but didn't answer. He did, however, follow me back to the house.

"It's awfully late for you to be out here by yourself," I commented as we walked along the cement walkway. "I bet your mom is worried."

"Ain't got no mom."

"Okay, then, how about your dad?"

"Gone."

"I see." I opened the back patio door and led the boy into the kitchen. I found a bowl for the milk. "So who takes care of you?" I asked after settling the kitten on the floor with her saucer and then began gathering ingredients for a sandwich.

"It's just me and Buck."

"Buck?"

"Guess he's sort of like an uncle, although he isn't a real uncle."

"I see. And where is Buck now?"

"Out."

I sliced the sandwich I'd made in half and set it on a plate. "Chips?" I asked, holding up the bag.

"Yes, please."

I set the plate on the table in front of the boy and then sat down on a chair across from him. "So do you and Buck live near here?"

"Sometimes."

"Sometimes?" I asked.

"Buck likes to move around. We've been camping in the woods not far from here. Buck's been gone for a few days and I don't like to sleep at the camp when I'm alone, so I've been sneaking down to sleep in the barn. Am I in trouble?"

"No, you aren't in trouble. If I were you I'd sleep in the barn too. It's warm and safe and it's nice to have company."

Tommy held up his glass. "Can I have more milk?"

"Absolutely." I got up and refilled the boy's glass. "Do you think Buck will be back tonight?"

The boy wiped his mouth with the back of his dirty hand. "Dunno."

I paused to consider what to do next. I'd said I wasn't going to call the cops and I wouldn't, but I couldn't very well send Tommy back out to sleep in the barn.

"You said there were three kittens. I wonder if the other kittens would like some milk."

Tommy scratched his head, which was covered with dirty blond hair, before answering. "I think they would. It seems like they're hungry."

"I think because they know you maybe you can help me catch them when you finish your sandwich. We'll bring them in and make sure they all have plenty to eat."

The boy looked at me with mistrust in his eyes, but then he agreed to my plan. It wasn't a particularly cold night, but it did worry me that the child didn't have a sweatshirt or jacket of any kind. Despite the warm weather during the day it did get chilly as the night wore on and I couldn't imagine sleeping outside without some sort of protection.

"I have a sweatshirt you can borrow." I held up a blue one I'd left in the laundry room. It hadn't yet been washed, but given the state of the boy's other clothing I didn't think that would matter.

"I'm okay."

"It's starting to get chilly and I'm not sure how long it will take for you to locate and catch the kittens. Maybe you should take it just in case." I handed it to the boy, who hesitantly accepted it. "In fact, I really never wear this particular sweatshirt anymore. Why don't you just keep it?"

"Are you sure?"

I shrugged. 'Yeah. I was just going to use it for rags."

Tommy slid the sweatshirt over his head. Given my petite size, it fit him pretty well. I grabbed the flashlight and indicated he should precede me through the back door. We crossed the patio and then headed back down the path to the barn.

"You said you were camped near here," I said as we walked. "Do you have a tent?"

"No."

"A sleeping bag?"

"Buck has some blankets, but I don't need one. The kittens are usually over near that pile of hay." Tommy paused and pointed. "There's a hole that goes under the barn."

"And they come out when they see you?" I asked.

"Usually. They like me. Sometimes I bring food to share with them."

We decided it would be best if I hung back while Tommy lured them out. The first kitten emerged and Tommy caught it and handed it to me and went back for the other. After we'd caught both kittens, we brought them inside the house and fed them.

"They seem pretty hungry," I observed as the kittens lapped up the milk.

"Their mom hasn't been around to take care of them for a while."

"Do you know what happened to her?"

Tommy shrugged. "Guess she just got tired of being a mom and moved on. It happens. When I first started coming around I'd see her once in a while, but I haven't seen her for days. Do you think the kittens are going to be okay?"

"I think they will. We can take care of them if their mom really is gone. Maybe they'd like to sleep in the house rather than under the barn."

"I bet they'd like to sleep on a real bed," Tommy agreed. He'd begun to relax. "Are you going to let them sleep on yours?"

"No. There's already someone in my bed."

Tommy nervously glanced toward the hallway. "The cowboy who owns the place?"

"Yes, him, and three dogs."

"The kittens don't like the dogs."

I picked up a longhaired black kitten and wiped his face. He sure was a cute little thing. The other two were just as cute. One was white and the other was gray-and-white-striped, but black kittens always had been my favorite. I glanced at Tommy, who needed to have his own face wiped. "I'm sure you're right about the kittens not liking the dogs. There's an extra bedroom just down the hall that has a very big bed. I wonder, if I had the kittens sleep there, would you mind staying as well to look after them? I hate to leave them all alone in a strange place. We wouldn't want them to be scared."

The boy stared at me. I could see he was calculating the odds that I was trying to trick him into doing something he didn't want to do. "You won't call the cops?"

"No. I already promised not to call the cops. I just want to have someone look after the baby kittens, and it seems like you might have time to take on a job like that."

The boy frowned and looked toward the hallway again. "What about him? Will he call the cops?"

"His name is Luke and he won't call the cops either. I promise. So how about it?"

"Okay. If you think it will help. I guess I can stay one night."

I smiled. "Great. How about if we give you a bath while the kittens finish eating?"

"I don't like baths."

"I can see that, but if you're going to sleep in a real bed with clean sheets I think it would be best if you were clean as well. I can give you a T-shirt to sleep in. I'll wash your clothes so you have clean clothes to put on tomorrow."

The boy frowned.

"Luke has a pool that I'm sure he'll let you swim in tomorrow, but only if you're clean," I told the boy. "There's a waterfall to swim under. It's really fun."

"I saw the pool and it did look like fun. I guess I can take a bath if I have to."

I made Tommy a nice warm bath and instructed him to leave his dirty clothes outside the door after he undressed. I left a long T-shirt I'd found in the laundry room for him to put on when he was finished bathing. I would wash his filthy clothes so he'd have something clean to put on the next morning. What he really needed were new clothes, but we'd figure things out as we went.

After Tommy was settled in the tub, I found an empty box and filled it with sand from the yard. As far as litter boxes went, it wasn't the best, but it would have to do. I just hoped the kittens would use it and not the carpet if they needed to relieve themselves during the night.

When Tommy was bathed and dressed I tucked him and the kittens into the guest room and closed the door behind me. I realized I couldn't keep Tommy indefinitely and had no idea what I was going to do in the long run, but for now the little boy and all three kittens were fed, warm, safe, and comfy. The blond-haired child was adorable once all the grime had been washed from his face. I wondered how he'd come to be with the man he'd called Buck.

I straightened the kitchen before heading back to Luke's room. I was surprised he hadn't awakened. He'd seemed sort of stressed lately but hadn't said why. It appeared to me that he hadn't been sleeping well, but when I'd asked him about it he'd said he was fine and I shouldn't worry. Of course not worrying was easier said than done.

I peeked in on Tommy again on my way down the hall. He looked almost angelic as he slept with all three kittens curled up next to him. I closed the door and continued on to the end of the hall, where Luke and the dogs were waiting. I stripped off my clothes and climbed quietly into the bed. Luke rolled over and pulled me toward him.

"Everything okay?" he asked, still half-asleep.

"Everything's fine." I decided to wait to tell him about Tommy in the morning.

Luke tightened his arm around me as I rested my head on his chest, listening to his heartbeat as I drifted contentedly off to sleep.

Chapter 5

Wednesday, March 22

I got up early the next morning to check on Tommy. As he was the last time I'd checked on him, he was sound asleep in the big bed with all three kittens sleeping next to him. I needed to figure out exactly what to do before he woke up. I'd promised I wouldn't call the cops and I always kept my promises, but I found I wasn't willing to let him return to a life with the obviously irresponsible Buck. Of course all I really had was Tommy's word that his parents weren't in the picture, so the first thing I needed to do was make sure he hadn't just run away.

Luke had gotten up even earlier than I and had taken one of the horses out for a ride, so I hadn't had a chance to mention that we had a houseguest, but I was sure he wouldn't mind. Still, I needed to figure out a long-term solution. I thought about calling Jason, but he was a cop in addition to being my brother, and his job would most likely require him to call Child Protective Services. I thought about calling my dad, who would have the knowledge necessary to look in to the situation but was retired and so might not consider himself bound to certain actions. Still, Dad did tend to be a by-the-books guy, so in the end I called my mom, who agreed to come right over.

"The poor dear," Mom sympathized as we shared a pot of tea. "He's much too young not to have anyone looking out for him."

"He said he didn't have a mom and his dad was *gone*, whatever that means. A man he referred to as Uncle Buck looks out for him, although he isn't a real uncle. From what he's told me, I have a feeling they're both homeless. I want to help Tommy, but I don't want to do something that will land him in a situation where he'll feel compelled to run away. I've only known him a short time, but I can tell he won't thrive in the CPS system. The kid has a real independent streak."

"Are you sure he's not a runaway?"

"No," I admitted.

Mom stirred some honey into her tea before responding. "The first thing we need to do is confirm what he told you. It's possible he does have a parent or legal guardian he ran away from for some reason, and if that's the case we absolutely can't harbor him. We could both end up in jail."

I sighed. "I guess you're right."

"I don't suppose he mentioned a last name?"

"No. I didn't ask, but I have a feeling he wouldn't tell me anyway. I wish I could stay home and look in to things, but I have a shift today and I know one of the other WSOs is going to be out, so calling in isn't an option."

"Just leave it to me." Mom patted my arm. "I raised six children. I'm a master at getting kids to talk."

"And then what?"

"I don't know. I guess we'll see."

"I promised him no cops."

"I'm not a cop and I think I can handle whatever turns out to be the truth. You can't be the wife of the police chief and not get to know a few people. Let's see if we can convince Tommy to come home with me. He can stay in one of your brothers' rooms until we straighten this whole thing out."

"What about Dad?"

"Dad's on Maui visiting with your brother for a few days, so we don't need to worry about him. Let's give Tommy some breakfast and discuss things with him."

Mom greeted Tommy with a maternal hug he seemed to respond to. She took her time and got to know him while she made pancakes for all of us. After Tommy had eaten she presented the idea of his going home with her for the day because I had to go to work. Tommy was leery at first, until we explained that Mom had both a swimming pool and a PlayStation she would be happy to give him unlimited access to. He seemed even more interested in the idea after Mom brought up the pulled pork she had cooking in her Crock-Pot. She assured him it would be just the two of them in the house and she would keep my promise not to call the cops. Of course she glossed over the fact that her husband was an ex-cop and all five of her sons were current cops, but they wouldn't be around, so it wouldn't be an issue. At least for the moment.

Mom also agreed to let Tommy bring all three kittens with him to her house, which absolutely amazed me because I'd begged for a pet as a child and always been turned down because animals were both messy and expensive. The fact that Mom was willing to go so far out of her way to help Tommy indicated to me just how lonely she'd become, or possibly what a good person she really was.

I packed Tommy and the cats into Mom's car and waved them off after promising to call later that afternoon to check on things. It occurred to me that helping Tommy was giving Mom a new lease on life. I just hoped things would work out for everyone.

******

I was assigned to the surfing beach that day, which was my favorite of all the tower assignments. It was a beautiful day, the sun bright, without a cloud in the sky. I was in the dispatch office taking a break after completing the first two hours of my shift when I got a call from Jason. I'd meant to call him the previous day to find out what was happening with the arm on the beach, but I'd become distracted by Vince Kensington and Shredder and had allowed it to slip to the back of my mind.

"Hey, Jason. What's going on?" I asked.

"Have you seen Komo Kamaka?"

"Not since last week. Why?"

"I went over to his food truck to ask him some questions about Blaze Whitmore, but he wasn't there. I went by his house and he wasn't at home either."

I frowned. "That's odd. Komo always opens his truck unless the weather's bad. Did you ask around? Maybe one of the other food truck vendors knows where he is. Or maybe he mentioned something to one of his regular customers."

"I asked a couple of the other vendors, but they all said they hadn't seen him since yesterday."

I glanced at the clock. Komo served breakfast and lunch and was usually open by seven. It was after eleven.

"Maybe he had an appointment. He might be planning to open later," I suggested.

"Maybe. I need to talk to him and plan to check back, but if you see him will you call me?"

"Sure. No problem." I leaned on the corner of one of the desks used by the resort's clerical staff. "What's so urgent?"

Jason hesitated, as if he wasn't sure he wanted to fill me in.

"Jason?" I pushed.

"I'm afraid Komo is the number one suspect in Whitmore's death."

"What?" I screeched. "Why?"

"Not only was he seen threatening Whitmore on Monday afternoon but we found a knife with blood on it in the trunk of his car. We don't have the body, so we can't know how he died, but death by stab wound is pretty common."

"Is the blood on the knife a match for Whitmore's?"

"We don't know yet. We're having it tested."

"Komo wouldn't kill anyone," I insisted. "Maybe someone is setting him up."

Jason sighed. "Maybe. But the knife, combined with an eyewitness account of him threatening to 'feed Blaze to the fishes' is enough for us to bring him in for questioning. It's probably enough for us to hold him too, unless he happens to have an alibi."

"He used those exact words?"

"I'm afraid so."

I hated to admit it, but things really didn't look good for Komo. He was a big teddy bear, but he'd been extremely vocal about his feelings toward the man who had been causing so many problems. "If you do track Komo down please give him the benefit of the doubt and the chance to explain things. We've both known Komo for most of our lives. You know he wouldn't kill anyone."

"I know." Jason sounded tired. "I really hope he can explain things. The last thing I want to do is lock him up, but I have to do my job."

"I can't help but worry."

"The best thing that can happen right now is for me to be able to find him and offer him the opportunity to explain things. Like I said, if you see him, call me."

"I will."

I returned to the tower and tried to get my head in the game. The waves were huge, as they often were at this time of the year, which meant the water was packed, requiring my full attention.

Unfortunately, I didn't have my full attention to give. Not that I was ignoring the water or in any way acting in a negligent manner, but I couldn't help but find my mind wandering to Komo and the mystery surrounding his disappearance. It bothered me that no one knew where Komo was. He always opened his food truck; not opening on a beautiful day like today was a very un-Komo thing to do. It also bothered me that he didn't seem to be home, yet no one had seen him around. If the knife had been found in the trunk of his car, that meant he hadn't taken his car when he took off.

There wasn't a lot I could do to look for Komo while I was supposed to have 100 percent of my attention on the water, but I had a lunch break coming in another hour, and if I timed things right I should be able to head over to the beach where a food truck owned and operated by two brothers named Buddy and Bobby was usually parked. They'd been friends with Komo for a long time. I figured if he'd confided in anyone it would likely be them.

"Tower two to base," I said, using my radio to contact the supervisor on duty.

"Go ahead," Brody Weller, a friend and fellow WSO, answered.

"There are three women just beyond the break line. They arrived on a boat but transferred to surfboards. It appears they're wearing mermaid outfits. Do you know anything about that?"

"Yeah. They're shooting a commercial. They wanted to do it as close to the shore as possible so they'd have the beach and the visitors in the background."

"Do you have a way to contact them? Two of the three mermaids are awfully close to the break. One early wave and they'll go under for sure. Real mermaids can swim, but I think the costumes the women are wearing will hinder their ability to do so."

"I'll contact the boat to let them know they should move farther out."

"Ten-four."

I watched as the women continued to float closer and closer to the danger zone. It seemed from where I was sitting that the people on the boat were more concerned about getting the perfect shot than making sure their models were safe. I used my binoculars to get the best visual I could. There was no doubt about it: the two mermaids closest to the shore were going to get caught in the breaking waves when they cycled through once more.

"Tower two to base," I radioed once again.

"Go for Brody."

"Did you get hold of the boat? If I'm right, the two mermaids closest to the beach are going under in about thirty seconds."

"I told the person I spoke to on the boat to move them farther out. I guess they ignored my counsel."

"I'm going in. Send backup."

Sure enough, by the time I jumped down off my tower, ran across the beach, and hit the water, a large wave had toppled two of the models. Even if the women were strong swimmers the outfits they wore were sure to fill with water and act as lead weights. I swam as fast as I could toward the last place I'd seen them. I was a strong swimmer and able to cover a lot of territory in a short amount of time. I just hoped I would be fast enough.

The first woman I came to had been frantically trying to get out of her water-filled tail. She had been submerged close to a minute by my calculation, so I needed to act fast. Luckily, I'd thought to grab the pocket knife I kept in the tower and was able to cut her free before she lost consciousness. Once we reached the surface, I told her to swim for the boat, took a deep breath, and went looking for victim number two. Unfortunately, enough time had passed by that point that it was likely I'd find her unconscious. Every second that passed decreased the likelihood she would survive, so I searched as quickly as I could. The water was clear today despite the surf, so I should be able to see her, yet I'd already turned in a full circle and she was nowhere in sight. Where could she have floated off to? I surfaced once again and took several deep breaths before diving back under. As I swam toward the ocean floor, I noticed the sun reflecting off something in the distance. The outfits the women were wearing had sequins to catch the sun, so I headed in that direction. By the time I reached the woman more than three minutes had passed.

I used my knife to cut her out of her tail, ignoring my own body's demand to breath. I grabbed her under the armpits and pushed off the bottom. By the time I reached the surface I was gasping for air. Fortunately, Brody had made it out to join me and was close enough so that I could hand her off. He performed mouth-to-mouth while we had her loaded onto the boat.

"There's an ambulance waiting at the boat launch," Brody informed the driver after we climbed on board. Brody and I continued to work on the woman until we were able to safely hand her off to the emergency medical technicians.

As I watched the ambulance speed away, I turned to the man who still held a camera. "What in the world were you thinking? Brody told you to pull back."

"I just needed a couple more shots. I'm a professional; I know what I'm doing. I've done dozens of shoots like this. That wave came out of nowhere. How was I supposed to know what would happen?"

"You should have known what would happen because Brody told you, you arrogant bastard. That girl might die because you figured you knew more about the behavior of the sea than men and women who have been trained to read the waves and make decisions accordingly. I pray that girl pulls through, but if she doesn't it's all on you!"

With that, I stormed away. I had executed hundreds of rescues in my years as a WSO. Many of the situations requiring rescue were the result of bad luck or unfortunate timing, and I could deal with that. But to put a woman's life in jeopardy for a lousy picture? There was no excuse for that.

When I returned to my tower another WSO had arrived. "Brody wants you to take a break. He said things got pretty intense out there."

"Yeah." I tossed my knife onto the counter that ran along the back of the lifeguard tower. "There comes a point where my tolerance for idiots reaches its limit. I have lunch in thirty; if it's okay I'll add that to my sixty and be back in ninety."

"That's fine. Take the time you need to unwind."

"Thanks. I appreciate it." Heading down the beach to interview two brothers about a missing friend was exactly the distraction I needed to get my head on straight.

******

Buddy and Bobby were transplants from Los Angeles. They'd grown up on the Southern California coast, and in many ways I considered them the quintessential beach boys often pictured when describing the California beach culture. They were both blond, with long hair, dark eyes, and deep golden tans. They spoke in the colloquial dialect that included more than the average number of *yo dudes* and *gnarlys* and when they weren't selling Dune Dogs and Buggy Burgers you could find them on the water chasing the next big wave.

"Yo Lani. How's it hanging?" Bobby greeted me when I arrived at their window.

"It's hanging fine. I wanted to talk with you and Buddy about Komo."

"Buddy's in the water. The waves are the bomb. You should head out."

"I'm working today, but I'm on my lunch hour. Have either you or Buddy seen Komo lately?"

"He was around a couple of days ago. Guess it must have been over the weekend. We didn't really talk. Heard the burger-for-a-buck guy ended up shark bait."

"You heard right, but it's Komo I'm worried about. He hasn't opened his truck today. That isn't like him."

Bobby shrugged. "I did see him hanging with the pack a while back. Not here; over near his truck. I don't know what they were jawing about, but associating with that group could have something to do with his disappearance."

By the pack, I knew Bobby was referring to a group most locals considered bad news. "Do you have any idea why Komo was hanging with the pack?"

"Naw. I guess he might have needed a job done."

A job like killing a man and tossing his body in the ocean?

Chapter 6

I still had thirty minutes left of my lunch hour when I returned to the resort, so I decided to head over to the lobby to chat with Kekoa. Talking with Bobby had helped to relieve the anger I'd been feeling toward the idiot on the boat, but it had also fueled my worry about Komo.

I had just found a place to park under a large tree when my mother called.

"Hey, Mom. Do you have news about Tommy?"

"Some," Mom answered. "I had one of the women I know from HPD pull missing persons reports and there's nothing fitting his description."

"That's good. I guess we can rule out kidnapping."

"Then I checked with social services to see if there was anyone fitting Tommy's description in the system. They're still checking, but the woman I spoke to assured me that no one meeting Tommy's description has been reported as a runaway."

I got out of my car and locked the door. "Are you sure you should have called them? I promised Tommy I wouldn't call the cops."

"Don't worry. I've only contacted people I know personally will want to help. If Tommy isn't already in the system I'm going to petition to be his temporary foster mother while we sort everything out."

I paused. "Are you sure? That's a big responsibility."

"I know. I've done it before and I know how difficult it can be. It's been a while since your father and I have fostered a child, so I'll need to renew my license, but I know people high up and am quite certain I can have things expedited."

I stopped walking, pausing under another large tree. "Speaking of Dad, have you filled him in on all this?"

"Not yet, but I will. I'm going to call him after I get all the details worked out."

I hesitated. Mom would be an excellent foster mother for Tommy, but I wanted her to be sure. "The last time you fostered a child Dad was still working and you had a couple of your own kids at home. Things are different now. Are you sure you want to be tied down?"

"I know most people look forward to retirement. They're happy when their children have moved out and are living their own lives. But I'm not most people. I've been miserable since everyone has been gone. I thought it would be better once your father retired, but it's been worse. For both of us. I raised six children and loved every moment of it. I don't want the luxury of free time or travel; what I want is to be needed. I didn't realize how much until you called me this morning. It appears Tommy has no one. He needs me. I want to do this."

"And do you think Tommy will want to stay?"

"I haven't talked to him yet, but he seems happy so far. The poor thing hasn't had anyone to rely on."

"Okay, but promise me you'll talk to Dad before you say anything to Tommy. I'd hate for him to get his hopes up and then have things fall through."

"I promise. The last thing I want to do is hurt the little guy."

I hung up the phone and continued to the lobby. I understood what Mom was saying and it did seem Tommy needed someone; I just hoped neither of them would wind up getting hurt.

"I heard what happened with the mermaids," Kekoa said when I arrived at the front desk. "You okay? Brody said you were pretty shaken up."

"I'm not sure shaken up is the right term, but I'm okay. I spoke to Jason earlier. He told me that he wanted to speak to Komo about Whitmore's death, but he hadn't opened his truck and wasn't at home. Brody told me to take an extra thirty, so I went over to the beach to talk with Bobby. I thought maybe he might know where Komo was, but all he could tell me was that he saw Komo with some of the pack a few days ago."

Kekoa frowned. "Why would he be hanging out with them?"

"I don't know, but the fact that he was worries me. Komo knows a lot of people and I guess those guys have to eat like everyone else, so Komo might have been with them to establish a relationship. But Bobby suggested Komo may have met them because he needed someone to do a job."

"What kind of job?"

"Something illegal. Something like murder."

Kekoa shook her head. "No way."

"Komo threatened, in public, to feed Blaze to the fishes if he didn't stop poaching his customers."

"I heard about that from one of the guys who hangs out on the surfing beach. And I do agree that saying that was probably unwise. But Komo is no dummy, and how dumb would he be to say something like that in a very public manner and then actually follow through with it?"

I hopped up onto the counter and sat down. "Pretty dumb, I guess. Still, it does seem like the evidence is stacking up against him. I understand why Jason wants to bring him in."

Kekoa opened the drawer beneath the computer and grabbed her pack of gum. She handed me a stick before taking one for herself. "If you don't want to make yourself nuts you should trust what you know. Do you really think Komo would kill a man?"

"No, I guess not." At least I hoped not. I only wished I could be as certain as she was. I'd known Komo my entire life and I knew him to be a sincere and dependable person. I'd been busy lately and hadn't eaten at his food truck for at least a month, but I couldn't imagine that enough had changed in that time to turn him into a killer. "The only thing that makes any sense at all is that someone who knows about Komo's beef with Blaze is setting him up, and Komo knows it and is hiding out. The question is, who's doing it and why?"

"The why might be to cover up their own guilt, but I have no idea who that might be," Kekoa said. "Maybe one of the other food truck vendors?"

"Maybe, but if I had a food truck and I killed a guy, I wouldn't frame another vendor. Doing that would only draw attention to food truck vendors in general. No, if I killed a man and was going to frame someone, I'd choose a person who was as removed from me as possible."

"That makes sense, but if not a food truck vendor then who?"

"I don't know, but if Komo is being framed I think the person doing it will turn out to be someone removed from his everyday life."

******

By the time I got off work I was tired and really wished I could just take a nap, but I knew Luke was about to be invaded by five seniors, so I went home, grabbed a quick shower, tossed some things in a bag because I was off the next day and would probably stay over with him, and left a note for Kekoa to call me. I was just attaching Sandy's leash to his collar when Luke arrived to pick me up.

"Thanks for coming to get me. I could have driven, but it's nice not to have to."

"It's not a problem. I just finished with my meeting."

"How'd it go?"

"Well, the man I'm negotiating with has a small ranch with only a couple of horses at this point, but he seems knowledgeable and appears to have purchased high-quality stock. There are still a few details we need to iron out, but I think we'll be able to work out a deal."

I yawned. "That's good."

"Tired?" Luke asked.

"Long day. I hope I can stay awake long enough to discuss wedding plans with the ladies. I still can't believe Janice is getting married. When she first announced she was joining a dating service I thought she was nuts, but she seemed to know what she wanted and she clearly knew how to get it. I hope it works out for her."

"Me too. I don't know RJ well, but I've had a few chats with him since he's been dating Janice and he seems like a good guy. At first I was concerned the twenty-year age difference would be a problem, but he seems fine with it. In fact, he seems really happy."

"I guess they're proof it's never too late to fall in love."

Luke grabbed my hand and gave it a squeeze. The remainder of the ride back to his ranch was a relaxing one as we listened to music and allowed the serenity of the evening to chase away the frustrations of the day. Luke parked in front of the house before getting out and opening my door. I laid my head on his shoulder as we walked hand in hand up the steps and through the front door. Sandy ran up to greet Luke's dogs, Duke and Dallas, who were in the middle of the happy dog dance. Once we entered the main living area Luke paused.

"What is it?" I asked.

"Someone's been here."

I looked around the room, which seemed to be undisturbed. "What makes you say that?"

"I specifically remember setting the alarm before I left. It was off when we came in."

"Maybe Brody was here." Brody lived in Luke's pool house and often came inside to steal a beer or scrounge for food.

"Maybe."

Luke let my hand drop to my side. He walked down the hall to his office. I followed behind, curious to see what he was looking for. He entered his office, paused, and looked around.

"Do you think someone was in *here*?" I asked. Brody would scrounge for food, but he wouldn't disturb Luke's office.

He glanced at his computer. It was on, although the screen was dark. Luke clicked it to reveal the desktop. "I'm certain I shut this down before I left."

"Isn't your computer password protected?"

"Yes. And my password isn't an easy one to guess." Luke frowned and walked over to the file cabinets. The first one he tried was locked. Luke accessed the key, which was hidden inside a book on one of the shelves. When he opened the cabinet, he said, "Someone has definitely gone through these files."

"How? The drawer was locked. Even I didn't know where the key was hidden."

Luke opened the next drawer. "I don't know, but the files have definitely been disturbed."

"Brody?"

"No. He has the alarm code to the house but not the password to my computer, and he doesn't know the location of the cabinet key. Someone else has been here. Someone with the expertise to hack their way into a password-protected computer and pick the lock on a file cabinet."

I frowned. "Okay, why? Is there anything in those files someone else would even care about?"

Luke didn't answer, which made me nervous. Was he hiding something?

I was about to ask Luke about the files when he received a text. He frowned as he read it. Then he slipped his cell phone back into his pocket.

"Who was that?" I asked.

"The man I met with today. He has a few questions and wants me to call him."

"Should we call HPD about the break-in?"

Luke hesitated before answering. "No."

"Why not? If someone broke in you should report it."

Luke stood in the middle of the room. He took my hand and pulled me closer to him. "What do you see?"

I looked around. "Nothing."

"Exactly. Nothing is missing. Nothing has been destroyed. The place hasn't been ransacked. The computer screen was off, although the hard drive was on. I remember turning it off, but I certainly can't prove it. An argument could easily be made that I turned off the screen and only thought I'd turned off the hard drive."

"What about the file cabinet?" I asked.

"Locked. On the surface nothing appeared to be disturbed. If whoever was here hadn't put the files back in alphabetical order I would never have known the files had been touched."

"You don't file alphabetically?"

"No. Chronologically."

"So you won't really have any evidence to offer the HPD that someone even was in the house in your absence?"

"Right. I've been out of the house all day. The break-in could have occurred at any time, so trying to determine who might have been in the area at a specific time won't help either."

I leaned against the corner of the desk. "What are you going to do?"

Luke logged the computer off. "We have guests on the way. I'll check on the horses and then I'll start the BBQ. Can you handle the salad?"

"Are you sure you want them to come? I can call to reschedule."

"No. It's fine. Whoever broke in is gone now. I'll change the password for the alarm system and move the key to my files."

I frowned. It seemed like Luke was taking the break-in pretty calmly. In fact, I thought he was a bit too calm given the situation. I'd be flipping out if someone broke into my condo and touched my things. Of course my things were such a cluttered mess, I'd probably never even know if someone had disturbed them.

After we left the office I followed Luke down the hall to the kitchen. The dogs were wrestling around in the main living area, which wasn't uncommon, but it did cause something to occur to me. "Duke and Dallas," I said. "Would they stand by and let a stranger enter the house?"

Luke frowned. "No, they wouldn't. In fact, they'd most likely attack an intruder they didn't know."

I looked around. "I don't see shredded clothing or blood or anything else that would indicate a dog attack. If the intruder made it all the way to your office, it must have been someone they knew."

Luke glanced at me. The look on his face mirrored my own concern. "You have a point. Who would come here and snoop around in my files?"

"I don't know, but maybe you should ask yourself what there is to find and who would have wanted to find it."

Luke glanced back toward the office. "The paperwork in the cabinets mostly relates to the horses, although there are financial files, as well as files left from my days on Wall Street. Those are all old. Useless to anyone really. I only keep them because I'm required to for ten years."

"You said you had financial files. Are you talking about your personal finances? Bank account numbers and such?"

"Nothing current. All my current banking records are on my computer."

"You might want to take a few minutes to change all your financial passwords. I'll start getting the food together while you do it."

"Yeah." Luke turned back toward the office. "That's a good idea. My financial records are double password protected, but I suppose if someone had the skill to break into the computer in the first place they'd be able to get past my firewall. I'll change the passwords, check on the horses, and meet you in the kitchen when I'm done."

******

By the time the seniors had arrived Luke had changed his passwords, checked on the horses, grilled the steaks, and was ready to serve. Elva, Janice, Tammy Rhea, and Emmy Jean all settled around the table near the pool and sipped the sweet tea I'd poured while Luke served the beef and brought out the salad.

"Before we begin talking about the wedding I wanted to let you know I got us a lead in the Blaze Whitmore death," Tammy Rhea, who was dressed in lime green capris and a bright yellow blouse, announced as soon as Luke joined us. "And it's a good one."

"Okay, what do you have?" I asked.

"It's not a what so much as a who," Tammy Rhea clarified.

"Okay, then, who do you have?"

"Ivana Whitmore."

"Blaze's wife?" I asked.

"Ex-wife. She doesn't live on the island. She divorced Blaze for infidelity before he moved here, but according to my masseuse, who I just happened to have an appointment with this morning, Ivana is here right now and has been for the past several days."

"And you think Blaze's ex killed him?"

"No better reason to kill a man than out of a jealous rage brought on by infidelity."

"Yeah, but Blaze was dumped in the ocean. That sounds more like premediated murder than a jealous rage."

"Being dumped is what happened to the man *after* he died. We really have no idea how that happened, right?"

Tammy Rhea had a point. A good one. The person who'd disposed of the body might not be the same one who'd killed Blaze, and even if they were, the death could have been an act of rage even though the method of disposal was intentional.

"Okay, but why do you think the ex-Mrs. Whitmore would come to the island and kill her husband now? I don't know how long ago they divorced, but I do know Blaze has been on the island since last November."

"In a word, Raquel Kennedy," Emmy Jean answered.

"And who is Raquel Kennedy?" I asked.

"Ivana Whitmore's sister and Blaze's most recent lover. Or at least that's the rumor that's going around. To be honest, I have no proof of it one way or the other."

I guess I could see a woman killing over a love affair between her sister and her ex, but if it were me, I'd be more likely to do away with the sister, and I said as much.

Tammy Rhea grabbed Emmy Jean's hand and gave it a squeeze. "The bond between sisters is a powerful thing that, in the end, no man can destroy. Take it from me, if Blaze was fooling around with his ex-sister-in-law, it would be Blaze who would ultimately suffer Ivana's wrath for his cheatin' ways."

"If the man was divorced what he was doing wasn't exactly cheating," I pointed out.

"Semantics. If the man hooked up with his wife's sister it was cheating, whether there's an ex designation involved in the equation or not."

The Southern sisters had come up with interesting clues. Unless Jason had solved the crime since the last time I'd spoken to him, I was certain he was going to want to hear about Ivana Whitmore and her presence on the island.

"Has anyone else heard anything that might relate to Blaze Whitmore's murder?" I asked.

"RJ said Blaze Whitmore has spent time in prison," Janice contributed.

"Did he know why?"

"He was looking into it for a story he's doing, but when I spoke to him last night he didn't have a lot of information, other than the fact that his stay was fairly short and he was pretty sure the conviction had to do with a white-collar crime. RJ thinks it might have been insider trading or embezzlement or something similar. Seems Blaze used to work as an investment banker."

"Blaze Whitmore was an investment banker? Why on earth was he selling burgers here then?"

"I suppose if he was convicted of a crime he might have lost his license, although selling burgers doesn't seem like the next logical choice. If I hear anything more specific I'll let you know."

I took a break to call Jason and fill him in on the leads the women had provided. As it turned out, Jason already knew about Blaze's ex being on the island, as well as his time in prison. I seemed to keep forgetting my big brother was a cop, and a good one at that. He might tolerate my nosing around in his investigations, but he surely didn't need my help.

"Okay, now that I've shared your leads with Jason let's talk about the wedding," I said.

"I spoke to RJ about having the wedding here and he's afraid, and rightfully so, that people he knows at the television station are going to be hurt if they aren't invited. What he suggested was that we elope as we planned and then come back to the ranch for a party with a very small group of friends later."

"That sounds reasonable," I commented. "As long as he can honestly tell the people at work that he eloped there shouldn't be any hurt feelings."

Janice nodded. "That's what we thought. And RJ wanted me to emphasis that we want it to be a small party. He'd probably be happier if we skipped it altogether, but he knows I'd enjoy sharing my special day with friends. This will probably be the last time I get married."

Probably? The woman was seventy-five after all.

"I think we can keep it to under twenty and still invite everyone who should be here," Emmy Jean said.

"Twenty or less would be perfect," Janice confirmed. "Are we thinking lunch? Because if we are, you should know RJ doesn't process beef all that well. Perhaps we could do fish."

I sat back and mostly watched as Emmy Jean and Tammy Rhea took over the discussion. I've said this before and I'm sure I'll have cause to say it again: The Southern sisters knew how to plan and execute a social event. They never seemed to be short of money, so I imagined they were well off, but if they ever did find themselves needing to raise funds they could certainly make a go of it as party planners.

By the time the seniors left, Emmy Jean and Tammy Rhea were in possession of notes outlining the date, time, menu, music choice, flowers, and colors for the affair. The idea of pulling together a party like this in a week left me feeling dizzy and I hadn't even been asked to do anything other than get Saturday off from work, which shouldn't be a problem because I had a ton of unused vacation time. Once we were alone, Luke and I headed out to the barn to check on the horses.

"I have to hand it to the sisters. They seemed to know exactly what Janice would like," Luke commented as we walked across the property.

"They really do know their stuff. The entire time they were planning the party I kept thinking that if it were left up to me we would be eating burgers off paper plates."

"An equally valid choice."

I smiled.

"When I was a kid I attended an uncle's wedding," Luke told me. "The bride and groom arrived on horseback. They dismounted for the actual ceremony, but then, when it was over, they remounted and rode off into the sunset. I remember thinking that if I ever got married that was exactly how I'd want to do it."

"On horseback? You must be kidding."

Luke shook his head. "Nope. I'm quite serious."

"In that case I think we need to break up."

Luke laughed. "Why? Are you afraid you'll fall madly in love with me, I'll propose, and I'll insist we arrive at our wedding ceremony on horseback?"

"Not even for a minute. I'm sorry to burst your bubble, but I can't imagine being in love with anyone enough to agree to such a cockamamy idea. Now a wedding on surfboards at sunset..."

"When you were younger did you dream about what your wedding would be like when you grew up?" Luke asked. "Most little girls do."

"Not this little girl. The only thing I dreamed about when I was a kid was being a cop."

"I guess that fits what I know about you."

"By the way, we've been so busy I still haven't had the opportunity to tell you about Tommy."

"Tommy?"

"A little boy I found in the barn last night. I saw a light and went out to investigate. Tommy was hiding in the new foal's stall, clutching a kitten."

I explained everything that had happened, including the fact that Tommy was now staying with my mother, as we entered the dark interior of the white building that housed Luke's horses.

"How's my guy?" I asked the huge black stallion with a gentle disposition who trotted over to me the minute I entered the barn. I handed him an apple, which he refused to take. "What's wrong with Lucifer?" I asked. "He always wants an apple."

Luke frowned as he ran a hand over the horse's belly. "I'm not sure. He's been off his feed for the past week. I had the vet check him and he didn't find anything wrong, but I'm starting to worry."

I ran my hand along Lucifer's nose and looked him in the eye. "What's going on, big guy? Do you have a tummy ache?"

The horse nodded his head, but I suspected it was more in response to my petting than in answer to my question.

"What are you going to do?" I asked.

"I've changed his feed and I'm going to keep an eye on things. He's lost weight, but not so much as to be overly concerned. If I have to I'll call my dad. He usually has good suggestions when I'm at a loss."

"I know you don't always get along with your dad, but he sounds like a good guy."

"He is," Luke confirmed. "We don't really see eye to eye, but that doesn't mean I don't think he's an intelligent, honorable man."

"I'd like to meet him someday."

Luke left Lucifer's stall and headed to the next one in the row. "My mom is pretty much insisting that I come home for Christmas next year. I know it's only March, but she's already recruited my sisters to join her in pressuring me into complying."

"Pressuring?"

"They've each called twice, and if I know them, they'll keep doing it until I commit to coming. The reality is that once my sisters get involved it's only a matter of time until I give in, and I did miss this past Christmas with the family. I think the real selling point, though, is that both of my sisters will have new nieces for me to meet by the time Christmas rolls around. I'd very much like for you to come with me."

"To Texas?"

"Yes, to Texas."

"Where they keep all the cows?"

Luke laughed. "There may be cows, and I know you aren't a fan, but there's also family and small-town traditions and, if we're lucky, perhaps even snow."

I would like to experience a white Christmas, and if my relationship with Luke was to continue I supposed it would be good to meet his family. It would be strange not to be home for Christmas, but my brothers had jobs and families that didn't always allow them to join the family celebration, so it wasn't as if I'd be the only one missing. And the traditions Luke had described to me last Christmas really had seemed charming and very different from the ones I'd known. But we were talking nine months from now. A lot could happen in nine months. "Can I think about it?"

Luke shrugged. "Sure. Just let me know."

He sounded indifferent to my answer, but I could tell he was hurt I hadn't jumped at the chance to visit his family and hometown. Luke changed the subject and I let him. We chatted about inconsequential things such as the weather and the upcoming surfing competition as he finished his rounds.

Every time Luke brought up Texas it reminded me that our relationship existed in a vacuum that, in my own mind, was bound to come crashing down the moment he realized his life was really back home in the state of his birth.

Chapter 7

Thursday, March 23

After discussing the situation over coffee, Luke and I had decided to focus our energy on finding Komo, who I was increasingly worried about. Our plan was to visit his food truck this morning and if he still wasn't there, we'd have breakfast at one of the other ones in the hope of picking up clues as to what had been going on with him prior to his disappearance.

We discovered that Komo's truck hadn't appeared for the second day in a row. Luke and I sat down at one of the picnic benches nearby to discuss what to do first. There were five other food trucks that usually parked in close enough proximity to Blaze Whitmore's to be impacted by his burger-for-a-buck campaign. I already knew Buddy and Bobby didn't know where Komo was, although Bobby had told me about seeing Komo with members of the pack. We could check with them again, especially because I hadn't spoken with Buddy, but we decided to start our search with Zipper, who I remembered had gotten into a fistfight with another vendor, Sarge.

Zipper was a rough-looking man who appeared to be in his late fifties or early sixties. He was tall, with long gray hair he wore tied back in a ponytail. His eyes were so dark as to appear black and he had a long scar down one side of his face that began at his temple, crossed his eye, and ended up just above his chin. The wound had left a zigzag mark surrounding the original wound that looked a lot like a zipper and obviously served as the basis for his nickname.

"What can I getcha?" Zipper asked when Luke and I walked up to his window.

"We're going to share a chili burger," Luke answered.

"Fries?"

"No, just the burger," Luke informed the man who wore a white tank top over faded jeans.

"Guess you heard about Blaze Whitmore?" I jumped in.

"Yeah, I heard. That'll be five-fifty."

Luke paid him while I searched for a way to engage him in conversation. I didn't know Zipper well, although I'd bought food from his truck from time to time. He'd been working his truck for at least a decade and while he had many regular customers, he didn't seem to have a lot of friends. He was a stoic sort who tended to keep his thoughts to himself. I remembered hearing he'd spent a good amount of time in prison before coming to the island, but I didn't think I'd ever known what he'd done to land him there in the first place.

"A lot of folks aren't sorry the man is dead," I added, trying to draw him out. "In fact, it seems most people I've spoken to are pretty happy with the way things have worked out. I even heard some people on the beach saying that whoever fed Whitmore to the sharks should be considered a local hero."

"I don't know that I'd call the man who freed us from burgers for a buck a hero, but I can't say I'm broken up about having him gone. Do you all want onions on your burger?"

Luke and I said we did.

"Did you hear that Komo is missing?" I asked as we waited for the burger to cook.

Zipper narrowed his dark eyes. "Yeah, I heard."

"There are some people who are saying he's missing because he's hiding out," I added. "They say Komo killed Whitmore and is running from the HPD. The thing is, I don't think Komo would commit murder."

"Guess you never know what a man is capable of when he's pushed. Cheese?"

"Yes, please," I answered. "I guess it's possible Komo could have killed Whitmore—he certainly had reason to— but my gut says he didn't do it. I know you have an ear to the ground. I don't suppose you've heard anything?"

"Nope." Zipper passed the chili burger through the window. "Napkins are on the side."

The chili burger looked delicious, even though it was only ten o'clock in the morning. Luke and I took it back to the picnic bench.

"Zipper isn't exactly talkative this morning," I whispered.

"Maybe *he's* the guilty party," Luke whispered back.

"Maybe." I glanced at the truck, where Zipper was serving another customer. "I wonder if we can goad him into telling us about his argument with Sarge."

"Might be easier just to ask Sarge," Luke pointed out. "He seems to be chattier. Zipper is pretty stoic even when he doesn't have something to hide."

"Yeah, I guess you're right. Maybe we should have just started with Sarge. Now we're going to have to eat two breakfasts."

"Sarge has a breakfast burrito with SPAM, rice, and eggs that's pretty good," Luke said. "We can share one of those. Two half breakfasts make a whole."

"That sounds good and I guess I'm still hungry." I looked out toward the water, which was sparkling under the bright sunshine. It would be an optimal day for surfing. Other than my short session on Tuesday, before I was interrupted by the sharks, I hadn't found the time for surfing in over a week. I could hear the waves calling me. "It just occurred to me that I'm spending my day off searching for a man who may simply have gone on vacation. Do you think we're wasting our time?"

Luke glanced out over the water, where hundreds of surfers were waiting for the next wave. "Do you really think Komo could have decided to take a couple of days off?"

I sighed. "Probably not. And if he had he would have mentioned it to someone."

"Have you spoken to Jason today?"

"No. I should call him to make sure he hasn't already located him. In retrospect I guess we should have done that before we wasted the morning looking for someone who might already have been found."

Luke placed his hand over mine. "We didn't waste the morning. I'm enjoying spending time with you, and we needed to eat anyway. Call Jason and see what he says. If he still hasn't found Komo we'll go see Sarge."

I pulled my cell phone out of my pocket and dialed Jason's cell number. It rang five times before he answered.

"Hey, Lani. Can I call you right back? I'm in the middle of something."

"Yeah. No problem." I hung up and turned to Luke. "He's going to call me back."

Luke stood up. Picking up our trash, he placed it in a nearby trash can. When he returned to the table he offered me his hand. "How about we take a walk while we wait? It's a beautiful day and I wouldn't mind burning off at least part of that burger before we head over to see Sarge for breakfast number two."

I took Luke's hand and let him pull me to my feet. It really was beautiful, and while I would have preferred being in the water, walking along the beach trail hand in hand with Luke wasn't a bad way to spend some of it.

There were many things I loved about Luke: his welcoming smile; his kind heart; his integrity; his giving nature. To my mind, he was a well-rounded, super man who was always there when I needed him, but one of my very favorite things about him was his easygoing way of approaching life.

"I suppose I should check with my mother to see how she's doing with Tommy," I said as we paused at the top of the bluff.

"Has she found out anything about his background?" Luke asked.

"Not as of last night. He hasn't been reported as a missing child or a runaway and he isn't currently in the foster care system. He keeps telling Mom he has no mother and his father is gone; he either really doesn't know more than that or he's choosing not to elaborate. Mom has friends who work with Child Protective Services who are helping her figure this whole thing out, but I imagine if they can't locate his parents or legal guardian, at some point he'll be forced to enter the system as a ward of the state. Mom is still hoping to become his foster mother if that happens, but the last time I spoke with her, she still hadn't discussed things with my father. I have to admit that concerns me."

"Your dad won't be on Maui forever," Luke said. "At some point he'll come home and find out what's going on whether she tells him before that or not."

"I think it'll go over better if she brings him into the situation sooner rather than later. Secrets in a relationship are never a good idea."

Luke frowned. "Of course I agree with that."

I turned and put my arm around him. We walked on in silence for several minutes before Jason returned my call.

"What's up?" he asked when I answered.

"I was just calling to see if you ever located Komo."

"Nope. We've checked his home several times, and all his favorite haunts. We've talked to his friends. It's like the guy disappeared."

"So he didn't mention to anyone that he might be going away for some reason?" I verified.

"Not as far as I can tell. I hate to say this, but the fact that he disappeared the day after a man everyone knew he'd threatened actually turned up dead makes him look guilty."

I sighed. It really did. "What if he isn't in hiding because he killed Whitmore? What if it's because he knows he's in danger?"

"Why would Komo be in danger?"

"If he didn't kill Whitmore, it looks like whoever did is trying to frame Komo. Maybe the person doing the framing wants to make sure Komo isn't able to prove his innocence."

Jason let out a long breath. "Komo needs to come in. If he needs one, we'll get him a good attorney. If he's being set up to take the fall we can protect him. Nothing good will come from his trying to deal with this on his own. We really need to find him."

"I'll keep looking. If I find him I'll let you know."

I hung up and glanced at Luke, who had a strange look on his face. "Is something wrong?" I asked.

"No. Nothing's wrong. I'm just worried about Komo."

"Yeah, me too. Let's go talk to Sarge. The sooner we find Komo the better the odds are that Jason can help him."

"Maybe Sarge will be a bit more talkative than Zipper," Luke said encouragingly as we turned around and headed back to the trucks.

As it turned out, Sarge, a man in his midsixties with a military haircut and tattoos on both arms, was in a talkative mood, as we'd hoped. We ordered the breakfast burrito, which turned out to be to die for. Unfortunately, the chili burger we'd recently shared was sitting like a block of cement on my stomach, making me wish we'd begun our morning with our second stop.

I opened the conversation in the same way I had with Zipper after Sarge brought our order to the table where Luke and I were waiting. "Guess you heard about Blake Whitmore."

"I heard. The guy was bad for the island and I'm happy to see him gone."

"My brother told me they suspect Komo."

Sarge's nostrils flared as he answered. "Everyone knows Komo didn't kill no one. Sure, Komo was madder than a cat with his tail caught in a screen door that Whitmore was putting us out of business. We all were. Who could blame us? But there's no way Komo would off the guy."

I paused. "I agree you all had a legitimate beef with Whitmore and I don't think Komo did it either, but Komo's disappearance makes him look guilty. Do you have any idea who did it?"

"If you ask me the guy was into something other than food."

I frowned. "What do you mean?"

"It just seems he had more going on than cheap burgers. If I had to bet I'd say carving out a territory for himself in the food truck business wasn't his end game."

"What else do you think he had going on?" I asked.

"Selling burgers at a buck, even if he was able to upsell some of his customers, he had to be losing money. Maybe burgers weren't the only thing he was selling."

"Drugs?" I asked.

Sarge shrugged. "Maybe. Or maybe it was something else. Don't know for certain. I talked to Shredder about it this morning when he stopped by and he had a similar observation."

"You spoke to Shredder?"

"Yeah. I just said that. He came by with Riptide for breakfast."

"Did he say anything else?"

"Not really. I mean we chatted, but it seems like you're interested in something specific."

I let out a short breath before replying. "I'm not after anything specific. I just haven't seen Shredder for a while and wondered what he'd been up to."

"He had his board, so I'm guessing surfing."

I smiled. 'Yeah. You're most likely right. You know me, worrywart Lani. So other than Shredder, have you discussed your drug theory with anyone?"

"One of my regulars thinks Whitmore was running a bookie operation out of his truck and Zipper thinks he was hooked in with organized crime. Of course Zipper doesn't know what he's talking about half the time."

"I heard the two of you got into a fight the other day."

"You heard right, although the beef between me and Zipper has nothing to do with Blaze Whitmore and his burger scheme. No, me and Zipper go way back, and our problems go way back too."

"I see. Do you know why Zipper thinks Blaze was involved in organized crime?" I asked.

"Let's just say the man's clientele was a lot more ethnically and socioeconomically diverse than you're likely to find at the average food truck."

"So even though he was selling his burgers for a buck he catered to upper-class customers?" I clarified.

"I'm not saying he didn't have legitimate customers looking for a deal on their lunch, but we all noticed there were some pretty nice cars parked near his truck. Guys who drive Jags usually aren't interested in dollar hamburgers." Sarge turned toward his truck as some teens walked up to the window. "I gotta go make a living. Enjoy your meal."

"So what do you think?" I asked Luke after Sarge had moved away. "Do you think Blaze had more going on than just selling cheap burgers?"

Luke narrowed his eyes. "I don't know, but it would explain things. Sarge is right; at a dollar a burger he had to be losing money on every one he sold. If he had something else going on on the side and was just using the food truck as a front that could explain things."

"I wonder how we can find out for sure."

Luke drummed his fingers on the table. It appeared he was deep in thought. "I really don't know. Whatever Whitmore had going on is over now that he's dead and his truck is closed. Any customers of the side business will have moved on. If we'd suspected something earlier we could have struck up conversations with his regulars, but it may be too late for that."

"It couldn't hurt to ask around to see if anything pops. Komo was seen chatting with members of the pack," I reminded Luke. "Bobby thought he might have been with them to hire them to do a job, but what if he suspected Whitmore was involved in some illegal activity and figured the pack would be in the know about whatever was going on in the area? Of course to confirm that theory we'd need to track down Komo."

"We could go to the pack directly to ask them what sort of business they had with Komo," Luke suggested.

"The guys who run with the pack aren't the sort who are going to answer random questions asked by random people. I know a couple of people who might be able to arrange a meeting, but it might be better to explore our other options first. We still have a couple of truck owners to interview and I can think of a couple of Komo's regulars who could be helpful as well."

"I'm game for doing whatever you think is best, but I should head back to the ranch to check on Lucifer first," Luke said.

"Okay, but can we stop by my condo before that? I need to pick up a few things and I want to see if Shredder is back. In fact, you can just drop me off and I'll meet you at the ranch later."

Chapter 8

As it turned out, Shredder wasn't at home when I arrived, but one of his next-door neighbors, Kevin, had seen him pass by his window earlier that morning and then leave the complex several minutes later.

"Did you talk to him?" I asked the large, casually dressed man who enjoyed cooking and sports of all kinds.

"No." Kevin shook his head of dark hair. "I'd just gotten up and was making coffee. Sean was still asleep. When I saw Shredder pass by the window I didn't think anything of it. He does tend to come and go on his own timetable. I took some coffee in to Sean because he had a flight today and needed to get going, and when I returned to the kitchen to make breakfast I saw Shredder pass the window again, heading toward the parking lot. He might just have been going surfing. He does that most days."

"Yeah, maybe." I took a sip of the coffee Kevin had offered me. "So if Sean has a flight why are you here? Don't you usually team up?"

Sean and Kevin were flight attendants who were away more than they were home.

"Working and living together was becoming too much of a good thing, so we requested different assignments for a while. I love Sean, but we were starting to argue over the tiniest things. I think this break will do us good."

"I know a lot of couples who find it hard to work *and* live together. Are you home all week?"

"Until next Tuesday."

I paused while Kevin refilled my coffee cup before I continued. "If you see Shredder again will you ask him to call me? Tell him it's important."

"I can do that, but why don't you just call him yourself?" Kevin asked.

"I have. Multiple times. My calls just go to voice mail and he hasn't called me back. I was actually getting worried about him, but if you saw him this morning at least I know he's okay. What was he wearing?"

"Wearing?"

"When he passed by. Did he have on a jacket or a T-shirt?"

Kevin frowned. "I'm not sure I really noticed, but it must have been a T-shirt. I've never seen him wear a jacket, so I would have noticed. I don't know that he even owns one. Why do you ask?"

"I saw someone the other night from a distance. He looked like Shredder from behind, but he was wearing a dinner jacket."

"Then it probably wasn't Shredder. I've never seen him in anything other than shorts and T-shirts since I've known him."

"Yeah," I murmured. "You're probably right. Did you notice if Shredder had Riptide with him?"

Kevin frowned. "I didn't notice, but now that you mention it I don't think he did. I guess that's odd. Shredder takes Riptide with him everywhere."

"I suppose if you only saw Shredder pass by from the window Riptide could have been trotting along behind him, so you wouldn't have noticed him."

Kevin shrugged. "I suppose."

"Thanks for the coffee."

"Are you staying out at Luke's?"

"Probably tonight, but I'll be home tomorrow."

When I returned to the ranch I headed to the barn to inform Luke that I'd decided to take the three dogs for a walk while he saw to the horses. Luke had ended up calling his father, who had recommended a course of action he hoped would help stimulate Lucifer's appetite. Luke currently had ten horses at the ranch that required quite a bit of time on his part. Sometimes I forgot that just because Luke didn't have a job outside his work on the ranch didn't mean his time wasn't occupied. The ranch was located high on a bluff overlooking the ocean. I preferred my spot right on the beach, but the view from the bluff was breathtaking.

Sandy was my only dog, so he loved to visit the ranch, where he could hang out with his buddies, Duke and Dallas. All three dogs trotted ahead of me as I climbed the trail to the highest point on the property. It was a perfect day for a hike, sunny and warm but not hot and not overly humid. I felt myself relax and enjoy the journey as I made my way toward the summit. I wished I could say my mind was relaxed and serene as I hiked, but the reality was I was worried, not only about Komo but Shredder as well. On one hand, Kevin had seen Shredder with his own eyes and Sarge had seen him as well, so I knew he was most likely okay. On the other, he'd been acting in a very un-Shredderlike way. Not that he wasn't usually mysterious, because he was, but in all the time I'd known him, he'd never once spent any significant time away from his condo without letting someone know he'd be gone.

By the time I arrived at the top of the bluff my thoughts had shifted to Komo. While I supposed I should at least consider that Komo actually might have killed Blaze Whitmore, I still doubted that was the case. Komo didn't own a boat, so if he had killed Whitmore he would have needed to borrow one. I tried to figure out who he would have gone to if he'd needed to dump a body. Komo had a network of cousins and other family members, and some of them probably had boats, so he could have enlisted someone he could count on to keep his secret.

I sat down under a large tree and looked off into the distance, wondering how Komo's family was taking his disappearance. Actually, speaking to one of his cousins might tell me quite a lot. If they were worried that Komo hadn't taken out his truck for two days that would mean they also had no clue where he'd gone off to, but if they weren't worried, it would seem to confirm my theory that he was hiding out. Komo's cousin, Pomo, worked at a bike rental place near the beach. Once Luke had finished his chores we could stop by there on our way to talk to the two food truck drivers we still had to interview. I knew Pomo and Komo were close and hung out pretty often; it made sense that if Komo had planned to be away, Pomo would know about it.

"Whatcha got?" I asked Sandy, who had trotted over with something in his mouth. The last gift he'd brought me hadn't been pleasant, so when he brought me a brown paper bag I took it gingerly. I slowly opened it and discovered it contained the remnants of someone's lunch.

"Where did you get this?"

Sandy turned around and headed to a wooded area. Just beyond the cover of the trees was a rough campsite. It was currently deserted, but it looked as if someone had been there recently. I looked toward the house, which was clearly visible from where I now stood. I was pretty sure I'd be able to see in some of the windows with a pair of binoculars from here. Had someone been spying on Luke, or was this where Tommy and his uncle had been staying?

I decided to return to the ranch to tell Luke what I'd found. He was on the phone in his office when I got there, so I headed over to the pool house, where Brody lived, to ask if he'd noticed any strangers in the area. Brody said he hadn't, but he reminded me that the bluff had an excellent view in all directions; chances were someone had hiked up to the top of the bluff and decided to spend some time enjoying the isolation. Of course Brody didn't know about the break-in. For some inexplicable reason Luke hadn't wanted anyone to know that the information on his computer and in his files might have been compromised. It seemed odd to me, to say the least, but I trusted Luke to know the best way to handle the situation. It was, after all, his home, his office, and his files.

Luke finished his phone call and I told him I thought it might be a good idea not only to interview the food truck vendors but members of Komo's family as well. We made certain the dogs had fresh water, climbed back into his truck, and headed toward Pomo's bike rental.

"Did you ever figure out what the person who broke into your office was looking for?" I asked as we drove. I'd been thinking about the break-in quite a lot since finding the camp on the bluff.

"No. I did a complete search of my computer, but I couldn't find any evidence that it was hacked. Either I'm losing my mind and did just leave it on or the person who hacked into it really knows what they're doing and didn't leave a trace behind."

"And the files in the cabinet?"

"The same. They were out of order, but I didn't notice anything missing. I've been thinking about the fact that Duke and Dallas wouldn't have let a stranger walk into my office. Maybe I really am losing my mind."

Luke seemed to have completely changed his mind about the likelihood that someone had been on the property. "Did you ask Brody about the house alarm?"

"Yeah. He said he wasn't home at all that day. I'm not sure this particular mystery is one we're going to be able to solve."

"I still think you should have called Jason. He could have dusted for prints. He might have found something."

Luke shrugged. "Yeah, maybe, but it's too late now. Besides, I've pretty much decided the break-in never happened."

I paused. "I don't want to worry you, but when I was up on the bluff I found a deserted camp. The view from the bluff into the windows was direct. Anyone with halfway decent binoculars could have been spying on you."

Luke frowned. "You found the camp today?"

"Yes. While I was walking the dogs."

"I took a ride up there yesterday and didn't notice anything."

"The camp was hidden in the trees. I wouldn't have seen it, but Sandy found a bag with a half-eaten meal and led me to it."

"I'm sure it was just someone who climbed up for the view."

"Maybe. That's what Brody thought anyway."

Luke slowed and made a left-hand turn. After driving several blocks he asked, "Are we heading to the bike rental shop near the parking area?"

"Yeah. The first one you come to. I don't know for certain whether Pomo is working today, but it won't be all that far out of our way to pop in. He shouldn't be overly busy at this time of day; most people rent bikes in the morning and return them in the late afternoon."

Luke pulled into the parking area, where he found a spot near the front. We both got out and headed toward the rental counter, where I could see Pomo, who was built like a sumo wrestler, wearing a bright yellow shirt you couldn't help but notice. Komo's cousin had an unusually outgoing personality. I didn't know him as well as I knew Komo and I wasn't certain he'd tell me where Komo was even if he knew, but it couldn't hurt to ask.

"Can I help you?" he asked.

"Pomo, I'm Lani Pope. Komo's friend."

"Oh, hey, Lani. It's been a while. I didn't recognize you right off. Do you need a bike?"

I looked around to see if anyone could be listening to our conversation. "No. Actually, I'm here to see if you'd seen Komo. He hasn't opened the food truck since Tuesday and I was getting worried about him."

A look of concern came over his face. "Yeah, we're worried too. The dude just disappeared. I spoke to his brother yesterday and he hasn't been home or called anyone."

"Has he ever taken off like this before?"

"Never."

"Do you think he would call you if he could?"

Pomo hesitated. "I'm not sure. We're pretty close, even closer than he is with his brothers, but he's been acting strange lately. We hadn't hung out for a few weeks, so if he'd planned to be away he wouldn't necessarily have mentioned it to me. I know the stress of the whole food truck thing was getting to him."

"If Komo hasn't been talking to you can you think of anyone else he might have spoken to?"

"I'm sorry, but I really have no idea. I wish I could be more help."

"If you hear from him will you please ask him to call me? I'm really worried."

"Yeah, no problem."

Luke and I thanked Pomo and then returned to the truck. I wasn't sure if my chat with Pomo had made me more or less concerned about Komo. The fact that Komo hadn't even mentioned to Pomo that he'd be away made me more worried, but if he really was in trouble it seemed he would have gone to Pomo for help.

"What now?" Luke asked after we'd both climbed into the truck and fastened our seat belts. "Do you still want to visit the other two food trucks?"

I paused before answering. It felt like we were on a wild-goose chase, but I didn't have anything more important to do. "I guess as long as we're in the area it couldn't hurt to find out what Roxy and Keoke know. When I first started looking into Komo's disappearance I was certain he was innocent in Blaze Whitmore's death, but now I'm not so sure. It seems like even if he was hiding out he would contact his family. I wonder if the stress got to him and he went off the deep end completely."

"I guess it happens. Although…"

"Although what?"

Luke hesitated. "Never mind."

"It's too late for never mind. What were you going to say?"

"I don't want to worry you."

"I'm already worried." I gave Luke a hard look, and then it hit me. "You think Komo might be missing because he's a second victim."

"It's really a long shot but it did occur to me."

I sat back in the seat. The sun had been shining through the windshield while we spoke to Pomo, so the leather seat was warm. It should have occurred to me sooner that Komo might be a victim, but why would the killer try to frame him first if he was going to turn around and kill him? Unless Komo had figured out who it was who was setting him up and had confronted him. No matter how you looked at it, this was becoming more and more confusing.

"Let's go talk to Keoke," I said. "We can't know what's really going on with Komo, so it seems the best course of action at this point is to continue to look for him."

Luke turned the key and started the ignition, then carefully pulled the truck out of the parking area and headed for the highway. Keoke's truck was just down the beach, so it only took a few minutes to drive there. When we arrived, Luke pulled into a spot in the shade. There was a long line at Keoke's truck, which would make a conversation about Komo difficult, but I supposed we could order a drink or small snack and ask as many questions as we could in the time permitted. Investigating a murder involving a food truck was turning out to be a fattening endeavor indeed.

"Keoke has a pineapple pastry that's pretty good if you don't want a heavy meal," I told Luke as we got out of his truck and headed in Keoke's direction. "He also sells really yummy musubis if you aren't in the mood for a sweet."

"Something light sounds good. I'm still full from the two breakfasts, even though it's been hours since we ate."

"Let's go with the pineapple pastry for now. Something sweet sounds good to me. We won't have long to talk with him, so we'll need to get right to the point and ask him if he knows where Komo is. If we get the sense he knows more than he's able to say now, we can come back later when he isn't so busy."

"How well do you know Keoke? Do you think he'll talk?"

"I know him well enough to engage in casual conversation but not necessarily well enough that he would share confidences with me. I guess we'll just initiate a conversation and see how it goes."

We got into line behind a harried-looking woman who was trying to control three children who seemed more interested in fighting among themselves than they were in the food she was in line to buy. She asked them repeatedly what they wanted and no matter what any of them said it ended in an argument. It was times like these that I was pretty sure I never wanted kids of my own. Some women were maternal, but it seemed

Kailani Pope had been born without that gene.

When we finally arrived at the window I greeted Keoke, a short, thin man with dark hair and eyes, and ordered the pineapple pastry and two sodas. Then I immediately asked if he'd seen or heard from Komo.

"I talk to him last week," Keoke said.

"But not in the past couple of days?"

"Afraid not."

"What did you talk about when you spoke to him last week?" I asked.

Keoke shrugged. "Surfing. Food. You know, just stuff. That'll be six twenty-five."

Luke paid him.

"Did Komo mention anything about taking a trip?"

"Nope. Didn't say a word about anything like that."

"Did he say anything about Blaze Whitmore or the food truck war?"

Keoke leaned in and lowered his voice just a bit. "Actually, he did. He said he had a plan to get rid of Whitmore, though he didn't say what it was. Napkins?"

"Please. Did he talk about meeting with the pack?"

"Nope, but I guess that makes sense. If you want someone gone the pack always seem willing to lend a hand for the right price. Of course Komo doesn't have any money, so I'm not sure how he arranged a hit on the guy." Keoke placed the hot pastry on the counter. "Next," he called out, forcing me to step to the side.

"The more we dig, the more I really don't like what we're finding out," I said to Luke as we sat down on one of the picnic benches a few steps away. "If Komo is guilty I don't think I want to be the one to prove it."

"Do you want to stop?"

I took a bite of the pastry, which really was very good. "I don't know. Part of me wants to figure this whole thing out and part of me doesn't want to know."

"The only one left on our list is Roxy. I guess we can see what she has to say and then decide."

"Yeah, okay. That sounds like a good plan."

Roxy was the only female food truck vendor in the immediate area, although there were quite a few on the island overall. She was a native Hawaiian and had lived on the North Shore her entire life. Most of the time she knew everything that was going on with everyone, which made her a good source of information. Roxy's clientele differed somewhat from the other vendors we'd spoken to because she served fresh seafood and gourmet salads rather than burgers and sandwiches. Because her customers were unlikely to want a burger for a buck—or any amount of money, for that matter— she hadn't suffered nearly as much as her counterparts when Blaze showed up and opened shop.

"Hey, Lani. I have an ahi salad that's to die for if you're in the mood for something light," the petite woman in a blue T-shirt and cutoff shorts informed me.

"That sounds really good." I glanced at Luke.

"I'll have one as well," Luke added.

"It looks like you're busy today," I offered conversationally.

"I'm always busy. Gourmet trucks are killing it on the island. At least mine is. I know some of the guys have been struggling lately, though."

"Speaking of struggling, I guess you heard about the burger-for-a-buck guy?"

Roxy nodded. "Everyone's talking about it. I hate to see anyone end up shark bait, but he was bad news. Lots of folks who'd been friends their whole lives started bickering after he showed up. If you ask me, whoever offed the guy did us all a favor."

"That seems to be the popular sentiment. I don't suppose you have any theories as to who's responsible for his untimely demise?"

"Theories, sure. Proof, not so much."

"A lot of folks think Komo was behind the whole thing."

"Komo? Nah. I would be surprised if that were true. Yes, Komo was very vocal in his anger toward the man. He had a petition going around to force him to leave the island. Not that it would have gone anywhere. I think the burger-for-a buck dude had connections. Komo might have been getting frustrated with his lack of progress, but he wouldn't have killed the guy. He's nothing but a big teddy bear." I was relieved to hear Roxy's assessment. Komo *was* a big teddy bear and it really was hard time to believe he would harm anyone. I felt like I was on an emotional roller coaster. One minute I was certain Komo would never kill a man, even one he was so angry with, and the next I was just as certain he had.

"I don't suppose you have a theory as to what Komo meant when he said he was going to get rid of the guy?" I asked.

"He didn't say."

"And you have no idea where he might be now?"

"Sorry. I really don't."

"If you do see him can you please tell him I need to speak to him? It's urgent."

Roxy shrugged. "Sure. Okay."

Chapter 9

We were halfway through our salads when Brody called Luke to inform him that when he went to check on the horses he'd found Lucifer down. Luke told him to call the vet, then jumped up and headed to the truck. I'd never been a fan of horses, but I found I was as worried about Lucifer as I would have been if the animal that was ill was my dog. During the past year, the giant black horse with the huge dark eyes had wormed his way into my heart.

"I hope he's okay," I said as Luke sped toward the ranch, exceeding the speed limit by a good thirty miles an hour.

"Me too. He seemed fine when I checked on him earlier. In fact, he seemed better than he'd been in days. I can't imagine what could have happened."

"Maybe it's not serious. Maybe there's a simple explanation for everything that has been going on with him."

Luke didn't answer. He didn't say anything, but I could tell by the tightness around his mouth that he thought whatever was going on was serious indeed. I wished there was something I could do, something I could say. But I didn't know the first thing about horses, so I just sat quietly and prayed that the black stallion would be okay.

When we arrived at the ranch Luke went directly to the barn. The vet's car pulled in shortly after. I knew I'd just be in the way, so as worried as I was, I went to the house. We hadn't taken the dogs with us that afternoon and I knew they'd need to go out for a run, so I changed into my walking shoes and headed to the same bluff we'd climbed earlier in the day. I was halfway up when my phone rang.

"Hey, Janice. What's up?"

"You have to do something about Tammy Rhea and Emmy Jean."

"Okay." I paused and waved the dogs back to me. "What do I have to do?"

"They've completely taken over my wedding. It's like I have no say in any of the decisions."

I should have seen this coming. I'm not sure why I hadn't. The Southern sisters were both opinionated and pushy.

"Can you give me an example?" I asked as I started up the narrowest part of the trail.

"The flowers, for one. I told them that I didn't want to worry about carrying a bouquet; that instead, RJ and I would both wear leis."

"I love that idea."

"Well, apparently the sisters didn't because the florist just called to confirm a huge order of flowers for the day of the party; several bouquets as well as flowers for all the tables."

I let out a deep breath. Partly because the news about the party was causing me stress and partly because I was out of breath from the steep climb.

"Why would the sisters care whether you carried a bouquet? I thought you were getting married at a justice of the peace, without guests, and then coming back to the ranch for the reception."

"That's what we decided, but Emmy Jean and Tammy Rhea have other ideas. They're planning a big do. I wish we'd just gone ahead and eloped and never agreed to this party."

"I'll talk to them," I promised.

"Why are you breathing so heavily? I haven't caught you at a bad time, have I?"

The way Janice said *bad time* I knew exactly what she meant by it. Ew.

"As if I'd answer the phone if it really was a *bad time*. I'm hiking up the bluff with the dogs."

"I see. So you'll tell them no flowers and no guests I haven't personally invited?"

"I'll tell them."

"If they can't find it within themselves to remember that this is my wedding and therefore should be done my way, the party is off."

"I'll make them understand."

"Thank you. RJ is waiting for me, so I should go. I'll call you tomorrow."

I hung up and slipped my phone into my pocket. I had a feeling my conversation with the sisters would have a stronger impact if I did it in person. I'd try to stop by to speak to them after work tomorrow. They did have a way of steamrolling over everyone when it came to social events, but Janice was right; it was her wedding and she deserved to have it her way.

When I arrived at the top of the bluff I sat down on a large rock and looked out over the sea. I knew if I waited long enough the sunset would be beautiful, but the hike back to the house was a long one and it would most likely be dark before I arrived. I found myself wishing I had thought to bring a flashlight. Of course watching a romantic sunset would be a lot more meaningful if I'd waited for a time when Luke and I could see it together. All this talk about weddings was making me think about Luke's idea of a horseback wedding. I'd hoped he was kidding, but somehow I had the feeling he wasn't. Not that I'd ever thought about Luke and me marrying. Okay, maybe sometimes. But if that was in our future it was a long way off, so there was no use worrying about the details now.

I glanced toward the house, which looked quiet. I knew Luke, the vet, and probably Brody were in the barn and would most likely remain there until any danger had passed. Waiting wasn't my strong suit, but in this case it was probably the most helpful thing I could do. I was about to head back down the trail when Duke started to growl. I paused to listen, but all I could hear was the rustling of the shrubbery in the evening breeze.

I remembered the camp I'd found and realized I might not be alone. Should I check it out? I glanced back toward the ranch and then called the dogs to me. I really did need to get going if I didn't want to get caught in the dark, and if there was someone lurking in the shadows it was probably best not to confront them.

I was almost back to the house when my phone binged. It was a text from Kevin: Shredder had just turned up at the complex. I hated to miss him if he was only stopping in briefly, as he had before, so I left a note for Luke, saying I was running back to my place for a few minutes. I debated interrupting him to tell him in person but decided that because I'd only be gone for a short time, the note would suffice.

I drove as fast as I dared and headed straight to Shredder's place when I arrived at the condos. The unit was dark. I knocked anyway because I'd seen his car in the parking lot, but he didn't answer. The sky had darkened by this point, but he might have taken Riptide out for an evening run, so I headed toward the beach. I didn't see him, but I knew he tended to walk toward the right, so I headed in that direction. Maybe I should have brought Sandy. Sandy loved Shredder and had a sense when he was nearby. He probably would have found him in a minute.

I was about to turn around when I noticed a figure in the distance. All I could see was a silhouette, but it seemed man-size, so I went in that direction. I had just passed an area where trees grew close to the waterline when someone grabbed me from behind. My instinct was to scream, but the person who'd grabbed me had put a hand over my mouth.

I struggled until whoever it was whispered in my ear. "Lani, it's Shredder."

I stopped struggling.

"I'm going to remove my hand, but you can't make a sound. Do you understand?"

I nodded.

Shredder took his hand from my mouth and stepped back. I looked at him and shrugged, as if to say *what the heck?*

He pulled me into the trees, continuing to speak in a barely discernible voice. "I need to meet with the man waiting down the beach. I'm hoping he didn't see you, but if he did it's important he doesn't know we spoke. Wait here and I'll come back."

"What's going on?" I whispered back.

"I'll tell you after. Right now I need you to be invisible."

Okay, I mouthed.

I watched as Shredder continued down the beach. I could see the man he was talking to gesturing and looking in my direction. Between the darkness and the cover provided by the trees I was certain he couldn't see me, but I suspected he was asking about the woman he had seen earlier who had disappeared so abruptly. I didn't know what Shredder was telling him, or what he had gotten himself in to, but based on his wild arm motions I suspected it was fairly serious.

I couldn't hear what they were saying, but it looked as if Shredder handed something to the man. They talked for another minute, then both turned and headed in opposite directions, Shredder walking toward me, the other man headed back down the beach.

"What was that all about?" I asked after Shredder joined me.

"We need to talk."

"Do you want to go to your place?"

"No. Let's just have a seat over there."

I followed Shredder to the rock, sat down, and waited for him to fill me in.

"I saw you at the restaurant. I assume you were following me, or perhaps you were following Kensington," Shredder accused.

"Kekoa told me she saw you visit the man in bungalow six, who she suspected was a fed. You have this whole mysterious past going on, so I was curious. I knew Kensington had a reservation at the steak house, so I went there too to see who he met for dinner." I decided not to admit I'd been in the man's room and had been hiding under his bed when he'd made a phone call referring to a new lead. "Why were you meeting with him?"

"He's just an old friend."

"Really?" I asked, a tone of doubt evident in my voice.

"Really," Shredder insisted.

"So where have you been all week?"

"Around."

"Around where?"

"Just around." Shredder let out a frustrated groan. "I know you're curious, but in this case I really need you to leave things alone. Digging around in the wrong place could very well get you killed."

"Tell me what's going on and I won't have to dig."

"Lani, please. I'm not asking," he warned, "I'm telling you to leave this alone."

"Telling me?" I said in a high, screechy voice. "Who do you think you are, my mother?"

He just looked at me. I could see he was considering the situation. At some point he must have realized I was never going to let things go because his expression softened into one of resignation.

"I'll tell you what you want to know, but you can't tell anyone else. Not even Luke."

I hesitated. I didn't like the idea of keeping things from Luke.

"Promise me or I won't talk."

"Okay." I sighed. "I promise."

Shredder sat down next to me before he began. "Kensington is on Oahu to investigate a tip he received that at least one of the precious gems we know were stolen from various locations around the world ended up here. His source indicated the gems were being smuggled into the States a little at a time via one of the surfers on the professional circuit."

I paused to let that sink in. Shredder's big secret had to do with a smuggling ring? "So Kensington *is* CIA? Interpol?"

"That's classified."

"And you're helping him with his investigation?"

"In a way. Kensington needed an inside man to check things out, so he asked if I'd be willing to enter the surfing competition being held this weekend and do a bit of snooping. I agreed."

"So are *you* CIA?"

"No. Not CIA."

"Do you work for someone else?"

"Not anymore."

"Who did you used to work for?"

"That's classified," he repeated.

"Why did you quit?"

"Several years ago my partner was killed and I was injured during an operation. After my partner died I realized life was short, so I decided to retire. Given the covert nature of the division in which I was involved, the real me had to disappear."

"What's your real name?"

"Classified."

"Are you making all this up?"

Shredder winked. "That's classified as well."

"Okay, whatever. The guy you just met on the beach...was that Kensington?"

"No, that was someone else."

"Who?"

"Classified."

I rolled my eyes. I had a feeling Shredder was enjoying our little game, but I'd come about to the end of my patience. "So is that it? You're just going to enter the competition this weekend and see what you can find out?"

"That's about it."

Talk about anticlimactic. I felt like there was lots more to this, but I wasn't sure what it could be. "If the only thing that's going on is that you've agreed to enter a surfing competition to help this Kensington guy out, where have you been?"

"Classified."

"I have a very real feeling you're messing with me. There has to be more going on."

"Look, I've already told you more than I should have. Please just let me do my job. Stop following me, stop following Kensington, and stop digging around in Whitmore's death."

I frowned. "Whitmore's death? What does Whitmore's death have to do with this whole thing?"

Shredder didn't answer. I had the distinct feeling he was regretting bringing Blaze into the conversation.

"He was part of the smuggling operation," I realized and said so aloud before Shredder could answer. "The surfers were smuggling the stolen gems into the country and Whitmore was fencing them. His food truck was just a front for the fencing operation. But why him? And why here? Why even smuggle the gems into the country? Sounds risky.

Why not just fence them overseas or wherever it was they were stolen from?"

"You ask too many questions, and in this case questions can get you dead. I need you to promise me that you'll stay out of this."

"The gems aren't being exchanged for currency, are they?" I asked, completely ignoring the frantic expression on Shredder's face. "The gems are the currency. Whitmore was brokering an exchange for something else. I'm right, aren't I?"

"I think this conversation is over."

"Whatever Whitmore was selling must have been worth a lot to someone to set up such an elaborate system. First the gems had to be stolen and then they had to be smuggled onto the island and then they had to be transferred to whoever had whatever it is someone wanted so badly. It has to be information or intelligence of some sort. I bet it's a threat to national security. It's the only thing that makes sense. Are you NSA?"

Shredder didn't respond.

"It really doesn't matter. How can I help?"

Shredder let out a frustrated groan. I looked directly at him, and he suddenly looked a lot more formidable than I'd ever seen him. It occurred to me that my quiet, easygoing friend was hiding a very serious and somewhat scary side I'd never known he had.

"The surf competition is open to amateurs who qualify," I continued. "The qualifying round is tomorrow. I have some vacation time saved up and I've been thinking about trying a local competition, so I'll find someone to cover for me at the resort. If I can make the cut I can help you spy."

"You're going to do this no matter what I say, aren't you?"

"I am. If you're a smart guy—and I think you are—I'm sure you'll realize it would be best to work together. Maybe we should come up with a plan to meet."

"I really don't like this."

"I'm doing it whether you like it or not."

Shredder groaned. "If you make the cut after tomorrow's qualifying heats we'll meet Saturday, before the competition."

"Okay. When and where?"

"Six a.m. at Turtle Cove. We'll meet on the south end of the cove, near the entrance to the sea cave. Come alone. And Lani, if you love Luke you'll leave him out of this. Anyone who gets involved is going to be putting themselves in danger."

"I'll come alone." I stiffened my spine and agreed to Shredder's condition.

Chapter 10

Saturday, March 25

When I'd first insisted on helping Shredder investigate the smuggling ring I'd thought qualifying for the tournament would be a cinch. It wasn't. Although I'd been surfing almost since before I could walk, the competition for the few spots saved for local unseeded entrants had been fierce. I'd had to give it 110 percent to even make it into the top ten, and when they announced they would be cutting that down to five before the end of the day, I'd almost given up completely. Somehow I managed to dig down deep and surf better than I ever had in my life. By the time the day was over I was completely exhausted, but I had a spot in the completion, which would begin midmorning on Saturday.

I'd decided to sleep at my condo last night. For one thing, I was so exhausted that I figured I'd fall asleep the moment I got home, and for another, Shredder's insistence that I not tell Luke what I was doing left me feeling awkward and unsure when we were together. He was busy taking care of Lucifer and I had to get up early to meet Shredder, so I called Luke on Friday night to tell him I wasn't feeling that well and would catch up with him the following evening.

I glanced at my watch as I sat on a rock and looked out over the sea. Shredder was late. He'd said to meet him at six and it was now six-fifteen. I'd noticed he wasn't home when I'd arrived at my condo last night and his car hadn't been in the lot when I'd left that morning, so I had no way to know where he'd been hanging out since we'd spoken. I tried calling him, but the call went directly to voice mail, so I texted him and then tried to quell my irritation at his tardiness. I'd thought a lot about who Shredder really was and why he needed to maintain such an incredible level of secrecy since we'd been together on Thursday evening. Although I didn't see why he'd have reason to lie to me, and he really hadn't told me anything, I still had the feeling that something about his story was off. If Kensington was on the island to track down a smuggling ring chances were he was with Interpol. Unless, of course, I was correct and the gems were being exchanged for information, in which case the CIA could be involved. Shredder seemed to know the man fairly well, so it seemed obvious to me that he was, or had been, an international operative of some sort. I supposed that explained a lot about the intensity with which he guarded his privacy, but I still had a hard time picturing the casual, laid-back man I knew as ever having a job that required him to show up in a suit and tie *every* day.

I glanced at my watch again. Six twenty-five. If Shredder didn't show up soon I was going to have to leave in order to arrive at the contestant registration booth on time. Yeah, I had over an hour before I needed to sign in, but I found I was nervous about both my role as a spy and my role as a competitor in my very first professional surfing contest.

The waiting was killing me.

I got up from my position on the rock and began to pace back and forth. I needed to think about something else while I waited if I didn't want to go completely insane, so I went over everything I'd been worrying about in my head once again.

First there was Komo, and the fact that he still hadn't shown up. If Whitmore had been fencing stolen gems, as I suspected, the person who'd killed him most likely would be associated with the smuggling operation. If that were true, why would he target Komo as the fall guy? Komo certainly didn't have anything to do with international smuggling and espionage, so in my mind his involvement at any level didn't make sense. Sure he'd been vocal about his dislike of Whitmore, but a lot of the truck vendors had felt the same way. I didn't see why Komo would stand out more than any of the others, though, thinking back on my conversations with Kekoa, when I'd said that if I were going to frame someone I'd choose a person who didn't relate back to me in any way, I realized Komo was the perfect choice. Everyone knew he had a beef with the guy, and looking into his actions and motives would in no way point back to the smuggling ring.

And then there was the bloody knife found in Komo's trunk. I'd never gotten back with Jason about the identity of the person whose blood was on the knife, but when I stopped to think about it I knew the blood couldn't have been Whitmore's. If he'd had an oozing, bloody wound when he entered the water, the sharks would have found him a lot sooner than they had. The only thing that made sense was that Whitmore had been placed in the water free of wounds only to be cut up by the coral, as we'd discussed at the scene on the morning I'd found the arm. When the flesh was cut blood would enter the water, alerting any nearby predators. Once one shark started to party it was inevitable that his buddies would want to join in.

The other thing that swayed me against Komo as the killer was the timing of his disappearance. If he had been the one to kill Whitmore why had he gone to work on the day of the murder only to disappear the next? If you killed a man and planned to disappear because of it wouldn't you do it right away? I suppose someone could have tipped Komo off that he was a suspect and wanted for questioning. It was also possible Komo hadn't disappeared of his own free will. I hated to even consider that possibility, but Luke had had a good point when he'd said Komo could have been the murderer's second victim.

Another glance at my watch: 6:32. I'd give Shredder five more minutes and then I was out of there.

The other thing that had been on my mind quite a lot the past couple of days was Tommy and my mother's absolute determination to become his foster mother. I could see Mom was bonding with the child, which would be fine except she still hadn't told my dad about him. I wasn't sure how thrilled he would be about doing the whole childrearing thing after so many years, and I suspected that was why Mom was procrastinating about having the conversation that was already two days' late.

As of the last time I'd spoken to my mom, the woman from social services was still working on unraveling Tommy's identity and who was legally responsible for him. There was a chance whoever that was would have other plans for him altogether.

Although my watch informed me that it was now 6:41, I decided to wait another five minutes, mostly because I still had plenty of time to get to the competition and it seemed silly to go home and risk waking everyone up for such a short amount of time.

When I wasn't worrying about Komo or Tommy I was worrying about Luke. The poor guy had a lot on his plate right now with a sick horse and a potential intruder on the ranch. He was pretty sure that if someone had broken into his office something would have been taken. I could tell he was still disturbed about the fact that someone might have broken into the house, although he was trying to downplay his concern, most likely so I wouldn't worry. While there wasn't any verifiable proof that there'd been a break-in my intuition told me it had happened. And if nothing had been taken whoever had been in the house had been looking for something specific. Maybe they'd made a copy of something on his computer or in his file cabinet.

I'd just checked my watch and seen it was seven o'clock when I received a text from Shredder, letting me know he'd been held up and would meet me at the competition. *Wonderful*. I'd gotten up an hour early for nothing.

Now that I was on my way to the competition I found the focus of my worry segued to the role I was to play in Shredder's investigation. I wasn't even sure what I was supposed to do. I guess I'd hoped Shredder would lay out a plan at our meeting, which he'd apparently been too busy to attend. What could he possibly have been doing that was more important than this? I tried calling him to find out where exactly he wanted to meet, but he didn't answer his phone. The beach where the competition was being held would be packed. It was going to be hard to locate a specific person unless a meeting place had been prearranged.

There was already a long line at the registration table when I arrived, so I fell in behind a woman I recognized from surfing magazines. It suddenly hit me how far out of my league I was. Of course my main reason for being here was to track down international thieves and not to win the competition. Still, I didn't want to look bad in front of the huge crowd of people who had gathered to watch.

I looked around at the crowd but still didn't see Shredder. He'd better get there soon or he'd miss registering for his own spot in the competition. I frowned. It suddenly occurred to me that Shredder hadn't attended the qualifying rounds the previous day. It hadn't seemed odd to me at the time, but I was sure he wasn't ranked, so he'd need to qualify. Perhaps the agency he worked for had secured him a spot in the competition without his having to go through the exercise of qualifying.

"Name?" the woman at the table I had finally worked my way up to asked.

"Kailani Pope."

She found my name and put a check mark next to it. "Here's your contestant packet." She handed me a dark blue canvas bag. "Everything you need is inside. All contestants must be gathered near the grandstand at nine o'clock. Next."

I took my bag and headed toward my Jeep. I hadn't brought my board and bag with me while I waited in line, so I needed to retrieve everything I'd need. I had a little bit of time, so I slid into the driver's seat and looked over the information in the packet. Where was Shredder? He really should be here by now.

Once I'd looked everything over, I got my stuff and headed toward the changing tent that had been set up for contestants. I found a spot to set down my belongings and then looked around for the man with the long blond hair who had to be here by now.

"Is that Lani Pope?"

I turned to see an old crush, professional surfer Kilohana Kapole behind me. "Kilo! I didn't know you were entered in this competition."

"I was a last-minute addition. I wasn't going to come at first, but then I decided it would be nice to have a reason to come home for a few days. Are you entered?"

"I'm one of the five local qualifiers."

"That's awesome. Are the others here?"

"No. Not yet." I wasn't sure how to explain to the man I'd once fantasized about marrying that I hadn't told anyone what I was doing today. I guess I could have told Luke and my friends that I'd entered the competition, but I was afraid mentioning it to anyone would lead to questions I was unable to answer. "You must be the favorite in a competition like this."

"I'll win. I need to go find my girlfriend, but maybe we can catch up later."

"I'd like that."

There'd been a time I was crushed by the constant parade of women Kilo seemed to have moving through his life, but now I had Luke, so Kilo's women didn't faze me in the least.

Shredder still hadn't arrived by the time we were all supposed to be gathered in front of the grandstand. By this point I was beginning to get worried. Had something happened to him? He'd been part of an investigation involving some pretty bad people if what he'd told me was true. Maybe he'd asked the wrong questions of the wrong person. I'd left my phone in my bag back in the tent, but as soon as we were done with the opening ceremonies I'd head back there to try to get hold of him.

As we were being introduced, I found myself becoming caught up in the hype. Suddenly I wished I'd tried harder to figure out a way to invite Luke, Cam, and Kekoa here without telling them what I was doing. I still wasn't sure how I'd managed to qualify; surfers who were, in my own opinion, much better than me had been cut. One thing was for sure: I most likely wouldn't have another opportunity to participate in a competition like this, and it made me sad that no one was there to cheer me on.

Once the opening ceremonies were over the first round of surfers, of which I was a part, were asked to gather at the landing area. The phone call to Shredder would have to wait. I hurried to the tent to grab my board and then back down to the beach. I noticed that most of the contestants on the pro circuit had multiple boards and people to carry them. Given the huge crowd, tracking down the individuals involved in the smuggling operation was going to be a nearly impossible task. Again, I had to wonder of Shredder had had a plan in mind or if he'd simply been going to show up and wing it.

*****

I actually did a respectable job during my first round. I still hadn't seen Shredder and had no idea what it was I was supposed to do next, so I made my way back to the tent and grabbed my phone. There was a text from Shredder saying that he wasn't going to make it but I should just enjoy the day and text him if I happened to overhear anything.

Huh? Text him? Wasn't *him* being here the whole point of *my* being here?

Now what should I do? I supposed I could call Kekoa, who was at work, and ask her to put me in touch with Kensington. She'd wonder why I wanted to speak with him, but I figured if Shredder and Kensington were working together he might know how to get hold of the blond surfer who I was going to kill the next time I saw him. I felt bad that Luke was missing my big moment and had all but decided to call him when my mom called.

"Hey, Mom," I answered.

"Hi, honey. I know you're at work, but I hoped you had a moment to chat."

"I just happen to be on a break. What's up?"

"I finally called your father this morning and told him about Tommy. I wanted to let you know right away that he's fine with helping the boy. In fact, he's coming home today to help me figure things out. Isn't that wonderful?"

"It really is." I had to admit I was relieved.

"I knew you'd want to know right away that things were going to work out. And I knew you'd want to know your father spoke to Komo this week. I know you were worried he hadn't been around."

"He spoke to him? Where?"

"On Maui. Dad went to lunch with your brother at the Grand Wailea Resort and they ran into him there. It seems someone paid for him to have an all-expenses-paid trip. He said it was a total surprise. Isn't that nice?"

I frowned. "Yeah. Nice. Did he say who paid for the trip?"

"Actually, it was your friend Shredder."

I barely had time to react to the fact that Shredder had not only known where Komo was the entire time but had arranged for him to be off the island before my group was being called to gather for our next heat. Shredder knew

Komo was wanted for questioning; he knew how concerned I was about his disappearance. Why hadn't he said anything? More importantly, what in the heck was going on?

Every contestant participated in three heats before any eliminations were made. I was supposed to be here to look for an international jewel thief, but at this point I'd pretty much decided to drop out of the competition in favor of hunting down Shredder and strangling his scrawny neck. But I decided to call Jason before I did anything else. I figured he'd be interested in knowing exactly where Komo was and who was responsible for sending him there.

"Hey, sis, what's up?" Jason asked when he picked up his phone.

"I just spoke to Mom and it turns out Dad ran into Komo on Maui. I thought you'd want to know."

My statement was met with complete silence.

"You knew all along," I accused him. I wasn't sure how I knew that to be true, but I did. When Jason didn't respond I added, "Why would you pretend to be looking for Komo when you knew where he was all along?"

"It's complicated."

"Complicated how?" I demanded, a bit too loudly considering I was in a public place.

"I need to go. I'll call you later to explain everything."

Jason hung up immediately. I tried calling him back, but my call went straight to voice mail.

"Something wrong?" Kilo sat down next to me.

"That was my brother Jason. He always makes me nuts. How did your heat go?"

"Awesome. I caught yours too. Your technique has really improved since the last time we hung ten together."

"Thanks. I'm not a serious surfer like you are, but I do try to improve my skills. I doubt I'll make it out of the first round, but I've enjoyed having the opportunity to compete."

"I noticed you've been hanging out on your own. Didn't any of your friends come to cheer you on?"

"Cam and Kekoa had to work."

"How about that cowboy of yours?"

"He's got a sick horse."

"That's too bad. I gotta get going, but maybe we can hang later."

"Yeah, maybe."

There was a time I would have felt like I'd been to the moon and back if Kilo had asked me to hang out with him, but today wasn't that time. Today all I wanted to do was finish my round and then track down the men in my life who, I suddenly realized, had most likely been working together against me. If I had to guess, both Shredder and Jason had sent me on wild-goose chases in a lame attempt to protect me from whatever was really going on. It looked like their plan had worked. I'd spent the first part of the week trying to find a man who didn't need finding and the past two days first qualifying for and then competing in a contest that, I was willing to bet, had no connection in the least to an international smuggling ring.

Chapter 11

Once I realized I had most likely been duped my enthusiasm for the competition faded. I tracked down one of the event organizers and told them I had a family emergency and would need to remove myself from the competition. Then I gathered my things and headed back to my Jeep. My first instinct had been to track down and massacre both Jason and Shredder, but I'd had time to think things through and realized they weren't likely accomplices, which meant if they'd been working together to keep me distracted, I could be certain something big was going on. The question was what?

Now there was a bigger question in my mind: Was anyone else involved? Cam and Kekoa had been at work all week and neither of them had been involved in my search for Komo, so I didn't think they were part of the plot to keep me sidelined either. But Luke... he'd been beside me in my investigation all week. So, was he a pawn like me or the evil mastermind who'd set this whole thing up?

I decided to pick up Sandy and then drive out to the ranch to see what he had to say for himself. It tore at my heart to think he might have been in on the subterfuge. How could he lie to me? Granted, I'd agreed to lie to him, or at least hold back information from him, when Shredder had asked me to do so, but in my mind Luke's betrayal was not only different but much worse.

The first thing I noticed when I arrived was a black SUV in the drive that I didn't recognize. While the vehicle could belong to someone interested in one of Luke's horses, I suspected it was associated with whatever plot was underfoot. I paused as I considered what to do. If Luke was in on things and his objective was to keep me in the dark as to what was going on, my best course of action was to sneak up on him and listen in on whatever might be going on.

I slowly opened the front door and was met by Duke and Dallas. They greeted Sandy with frolicking doggy energy that I knew would alert Luke and whoever he was with to my presence, so I called them out onto the porch and then led them all to the closed-in pen Luke used to detain the dogs when customers came to the ranch. I went back to the house and let myself in through the front door. I didn't immediately see anyone, but I suspected Luke would most likely be in his office. I walked very slowly thought the living area, being careful not to make a sound, and then I slipped silently down the hallway. When I arrived at the door to Luke's office I leaned in and placed my ear against it. I couldn't make out everything that was being said, but I could hear at least two distinct voices inside, one of which belonged to Luke.

I quietly went to the kitchen and got a glass. I'd never tried the glass-against-the-wall trick, but I'd seen it done on television enough times to know how it was supposed to be done: putting a glass up to the wall and then listening from the other end was supposed to amplify sound. I wasn't sure it would work, but I couldn't hear clearly without it, so I didn't have anything to lose by trying. As it turned out, it worked a lot better than I'd hoped or imagined.

"This is your last chance to cooperate," a deep voice said.

There was a pause and then Luke responded. "I told you, I don't have the records you want. They don't exist. They never did."

My heart pounded in my chest as I tried to make sense of what I was hearing.

"And I told you I don't believe you. I never have." I heard a loud crash. Something either had been thrown to the floor or it fell. "Now, where are the documents?"

I immediately thought of the break-in Luke had suspected might have occurred. Mr. Deep Voice must be the one who'd broken in and tampered with Luke's files and computer. I couldn't see into the office to know exactly what was going on, but my sense was that Luke was in trouble, so I reached into my pocket and pulled out my phone. I had just dialed the 9 in 911 when someone came up behind me, grabbed me, and covered my mouth with a hand. I tried to struggle, but I felt myself being pulled helplessly away from the office and toward the front of the house. My assailant continued to propel me against my will until we were all the way in the kitchen.

It was at that point that Shredder whispered in my ear. "Don't make a sound."

I rolled my eyes upward as if by doing so I could see behind me. Of course it didn't work.

"M-m-m—" I tried to say against his hand.

Shredder clamped down even harder. "I need you to listen to me. I'll take away my hand, but you really can't make a sound. Do you understand?"

I nodded.

He slowly removed his hand from my mouth, although I sensed he was prepared to replace it if I didn't follow his instructions.

What's going on? I mouthed.

"It's a long story and I can't explain it right now. I need you to *quietly* go out to the barn and wait for me there."

"It sounds like Luke is in trouble," I whispered. "We need to call HPD."

"They're already here."

I looked around. I certainly didn't see anyone. "Where?"

"I have to get back. I need you to do as I say. Go out through the kitchen door as quietly as you can. Go around to the barn and wait there."

I hesitated.

"Now!" Shredder said in a very quiet but extremely demanding way.

I was startled by the serious tone in his voice, which caused me to take a step back before I nodded and headed to the kitchen door. Wow. Sweet, mild-mannered Shredder could look and sound like a serial killer if he wanted to. Not that I knew what serial killers looked and sounded like, but when he wanted to send a message of intimidation Shredder certainly knew how to pull it off.

Once I was out of the house I hesitated. Shredder had told me to go to the barn, but I really wanted to find out what was going on in Luke's office. I had a very bad feeling about things. If Luke was in trouble I needed to get help. At this point I wasn't sure if Shredder was working with the good guys or the bad ones. The thought that he might be one of the bad guys himself left me with a feeling of dread in the pit of my stomach.

I paused for just a moment and then headed around the house toward the back. There was a window in Luke's office that looked out onto an area where dense shrubbery grew. If I was quiet I could sneak around and look into the office window without Shredder or anyone else knowing what I was doing.

I moved as quietly as I could, first around to the back and then through the shrubbery toward the far side, where Luke's office was located. I walked slowly, happy I'd slipped on tennis shoes as the sound of something crunching beneath my feet penetrated the silence of the afternoon.

My arms and legs were scratched from my journey through the shrubs by the time I made it far enough around the house to see into Luke's office. I gasped at the scene playing out before my eyes. Luke was tied to a chair near the middle of the room. There was a trail of blood running down his face that looked as if it originated at his temple. The man I knew as Vince Kensington was gesturing wildly, yelling something I couldn't understand, while Shredder stood near the doorway with a gun in his hand. A gun that was pointed directly at Luke's head.

I covered my mouth with my hand to keep from letting out a scream. He'd lied to me! In the past I'd suspected Shredder was working with Kensington, but until this moment I'd never really believed it. Based on what I could see now and what I'd overheard a few minutes before, I thought Shredder must be working with Kensington to get something from Luke that he either really didn't have or wasn't willing to give up. I once again reached into my pocket for my phone, only to realize I no longer had it. Shredder must have taken it from me when he grabbed me.

I turned and looked back through the closed window. I felt like I was trapped in a nightmare in which nothing made sense. Despite the evidence of my own eyes, I was having a hard time believing Shredder was really helping Kensington.

I needed to get to a phone. I needed to call Jason; no matter what Shredder had said, he wasn't here. I was about to move back through the shrubs when Shredder handed the gun he was holding to Kensington and left the room. I frowned. I couldn't imagine where he was going. Kensington turned and pointed the gun at Luke. I felt my throat close with fear when he lifted the gun and pointed it at Luke's head. Kensington asked him something and Luke simply shook his head. I knew it was in my best interest to remain silent, but I couldn't help but scream when Kensington raised the weapon and the sound of a gunshot filled the air.

At this point rational thought fled from my mind completely. I ran from my hiding place and headed toward the kitchen door as fast as my legs would carry me. I had just turned the corner from the side to the back of the house when my five-foot-nothing frame rammed full force into a rock-solid body at least a foot taller than me.

I fell backward slightly and would most likely have fallen to the ground without the strong arms that steadied me.

"You killed him," I screamed at Shredder, tears streaming down my face. "You killed Luke!"

"I didn't kill Luke."

"I saw you. Kensington pulled the trigger, but I saw you with him. Why would you do it?"

I struggled to break free, but Shredder tightened his grip on my arms.

"Let me go," I screamed as my foot shot out and kicked him.

"Lani, stop!"

I paused.

"Luke isn't dead. I swear to you. Stop struggling and let me explain."

"Explain?" The man was insane. How in the world was he going to explain the scene I'd witnessed with my own eyes? I was preparing to kick Shredder again when I heard the sound of running feet. I looked at Shredder who, without releasing his hold on my arms, took me around the back of the house, where I could see uniformed men running through Luke's house to the office.

I glanced up at Shredder, who still had a death grip on me. "What's going on?"

"I'll explain everything. I promise. I need you to wait here by the pool."

"Like hell."

"Lani, please." Shredder looked pained. "I swear to you, Luke is fine. He's not dead. In fact, other than the cut on his head he isn't hurt at all."

"But I saw Kensington shoot him."

"With my gun."

I frowned. Was that supposed to make it better?

"Which was filled with blanks," Shredder finished.

"Blanks? Why?"

"Please. Just wait here. Give me five minutes and I'll come back and answer all your questions."

Shredder led me to a patio chair. He used his finger to wipe a tear from my eye before telling me one more time to stay put. Then he went back into the house. By this time there were HPD everywhere. My mind was screaming at me to get up to see what was going on, but still I waited. After what seemed like an eternity but was probably only a minute, Luke walked out onto the patio. I jumped up and ran into his outstretched arms.

"Oh my God. You're alive."

Luke pulled me hard against his chest as I sobbed in relief.

"I'm sorry," he said. "You weren't supposed to be here."

I pulled back slightly, narrowed my gaze, and looked Luke in the eye. "Not supposed to be here?"

Luke had been in on it. I still wasn't sure what *it* was, but Jason, Shredder, and Luke had all lied to me. I felt a piercing pain in my heart as I looked at Luke in disbelief. "How could you do this?"

"I'm sorry. I hated to lie to you, but I didn't want you to get hurt."

My gaze hardened. "*You* didn't want *me* to get hurt? Seems to me that you're the one who ended up hurt."

"I'm fine, really. It's over now. You're safe. We both are."

I took a step back and looked Luke directly in the eye. "I don't need you or anyone else to protect me. I'm a very capable woman who isn't a child and therefore is able to make her own decisions. I don't know what your idea of a partnership is, but I don't want to be in a relationship with someone who thinks so little of me that he has to lie to me. If you truly care about me, you'll stay away from me. I never want to speak to you again."

I fought to control my tears as I turned around and headed back to my Jeep.

Chapter 12

As soon as I arrived home I took a hot bath to relieve the burns on my arms and legs from the scratches I'd received when I'd worked my way through the shrubs. Then I dressed in a pair of jeans and a light sweatshirt, poured myself a glass of wine, and headed out onto the lanai. Neither Kekoa nor Cam were home, which was just as well because I was sure I wouldn't feel like talking to anyone ever again.

In all the confusion I'd forgotten Sandy, which meant I was going to have to go back to Luke's at some point to get him. On second thought, I'd just call Brody to ask him to bring him to me. I couldn't remember the last time I'd felt so betrayed. I was used to Jason treating me like a child but Luke? My heart bled when I thought of what I'd lost. Though if Luke felt he couldn't trust me enough to treat me like an equal, perhaps I'd never had him in the first place.

I looked up when Shredder, who seemed to come from nowhere, sat down next to me.

"I don't want to talk to you."

"So you don't want to know what was going on?"

I paused. "Okay, you can tell me what was going on, but that's it. Once you've done that I never want to speak to you again."

Shredder reached out to tuck a lock of my long dark hair behind my ear. Then he used a finger under my chin to turn my head so I was facing him. I felt tears stream down my face as he looked at me with something that mimicked sincere apology and compassion.

"I'm sorry for the way things worked out," he said in a steady voice. "But I'm not going to apologize. I did what I did to keep you safe and confronted with the same decision to make, I'd do it all over again."

I just looked at him. Traitorous tears continued to stream down my face as I fought for an expression of indifference.

"Vince Kensington is not only a very dangerous man, he's also a very disturbed one. He's little better than a serial killer who hides behind the authority others have granted him."

I frowned. "He's CIA?"

"Kensington is, or at least was, a member of the FBI. He was part of a task force that investigated white-collar crimes, but he was put on indefinite leave a while back after his methods were brought into question. I recognized him when he showed up on the island, so I called a former boss of mine. He asked me to find out what Kensington was up to. The day Kekoa saw me at the resort wasn't the first time I'd visited him."

"So you were a fed but you're no longer one?" I attempted to clarify.

"No, not a fed. But that isn't important. What's important is that after a bit of digging I found out that Kensington had come to the island after receiving a tip that Whitmore was here. You see, the men had a history."

"History?"

"Blaze Whitmore had been linked to dirty dealings for quite some time, though somehow he'd always managed to distance himself from the outcome. Kensington had been trying to find the evidence to put a nail in his coffin for a very long time."

I frowned. "I thought Whitmore had gone to prison."

"He did, but as far as Kensington was concerned, he'd gotten off too easy." Shredder hesitated and then continued. "Kensington's parents lost their lives' savings in a Ponzi scheme a while back. Kensington's father committed suicide after he lost his money and his mother sank into such a deep depression that she had to be institutionalized. Kensington transferred to the white-collar division of the FBI so he could personally investigate the case. At that time Whitmore was linked to the company that orchestrated the Ponzi scheme, but only in a very minor way. Kensington, however, believed he was the brains behind the whole thing. The problem was, he could never find the proof he needed. Whitmore was charged with a lesser crime and served two years in a very comfortable white-collar prison rather than being held responsible for the hundreds of millions of dollars that had been embezzled."

"I can see that would have made Kensington mad."

"Mad is putting it lightly. When Whitmore turned up on the island and opened the burger truck, Kensington was certain it was simply a way to launder the money he had hidden away. He followed him here to prove his theory and find the money. I met with him on Monday evening and he told me that he'd hit a dead end with Whitmore. You found Whitmore's arm on the beach on Tuesday morning."

"You think Kensington killed him?"

"I'm certain of it. Three other men have had accidents or turned up missing while Kensington was investigating them. That's the reason he was put on leave, pending an investigation into his methods."

"If Kensington has killed these people why doesn't the FBI just arrest him?"

"He's careful. No one has been able to find any proof that he's done what he's suspected of."

I took a minute to let that digest. There was a cool breeze that felt good against my dry skin. "I think I'm following you so far, but Blaze Whitmore is dead and both times you were seen with Kensington at the resort were after I found his arm. Why was Kensington still here, why were you continuing to meet with him, and what did Luke have to do with any of this?"

"Kensington stumbled on to a second target while he was on the island."

"A second target?"

"A second person he felt had gotten away with a crime he'd committed."

"And who was this person?"

"Luke."

"What? Why on earth would he be after Luke?" Even as I asked the question I knew what Shredder was telling me must be true. I'd seen Kensington pointing the gun at Luke. I'd heard him demanding papers.

Shredder looked away, then took a deep breath that he let out slowly. I could tell this conversation was making him very uncomfortable and I wondered if he'd continue.

"Shredder, why was Kensington investigating Luke?"

"I guess you know about Luke's past?"

"I know he was born in Texas and raised on a ranch. I know he has two brothers and two sisters, a mother who wants him to marry and have sons, and a father who wants him to raise cows. Despite his father's wishes, he moved to New York and took a job as a stockbroker after he graduated college. He did very well at it, made a lot of money, and retired after only a few years. He moved to Hawaii and bought a horse ranch. How am I doing so far?"

"Great."

"Okay, so what's with the FBI? I haven't mentioned a single thing that would get a person investigated."

Shredder paused but only briefly. "There were individuals in the FBI, like Kensington, who believed Luke didn't make his fortune legally. Or at least not completely legally. He seemed to have a knack for deciding when to buy and sell specific stocks that was so incredible, they believed he had access to inside information."

"The FBI thinks Luke was involved in insider trading?"

"A very quiet investigation was opened to study Luke's trades. So quiet I'm not sure Luke even knew he was being investigated. I looked into it a bit and I know he was sent some forms asking for specific information, but Kensington and the agents working for him wanted to be sure they had what they needed before they alerted him as to what was going on."

"Are you saying Luke is the subject of an open investigation?"

"No. The initial inquiry didn't turn up anything and he has since been cleared, but Kensington, as I've indicated, had totally gone off the deep end. He most likely would have continued to investigate

Luke after he was cleared, but then he disappeared."

I remembered Luke telling me that after he made his fortune he quit his job and traveled the world, never staying in one place very long.

"In Kensington's mind, Luke wasn't simply on vacation. He felt he'd intentionally disappeared to avoid prosecution. Luke swears he took off out of a need to put some distance between himself and a lifestyle that was choking the life out of him. I believe him, but Kensington didn't. He continued to try to track Luke down for quite some time. Eventually, he gave up."

"But then he saw him on Oahu when he was here to investigate Whitmore and jumped right back in where he'd left off," I supplied.

"Basically."

"And you were helping him?"

"No. Not helping. I was actually putting Kensington in a position where I could get the proof I needed to help put him away."

My eyes grew ten sizes when the light bulb went on. "You used Luke as bait!"

"I did."

"He could have been killed."

"He wasn't ever in any real danger. I was with Kensington the entire time."

I frowned as I tried to work things through in my head. "Luke knew you sent Komo to Maui so I would spend the whole week looking for him, therefore staying out of your way?"

"Not at first, but yeah, eventually I explained everything to him."

"When?"

"Wednesday afternoon, after he realized his office had been broken in to."

If Shredder was with Kensington when he broke into Luke's office I supposed that explained why they dogs didn't go all Cujo on the intruder. Duke and Dallas adored Shredder. "The text he received was from you, not from a man interested in a horse?"

Shredder nodded. "It's not his fault he didn't tell you. I swore him to secrecy. We didn't want anyone to do or say anything to tip Kensington off. He had to believe Luke was guilty and that I was helping him prove it."

I let out a long breath. "You knew Kensington would try to kill Luke if he didn't get the proof he needed."

"We hoped he would."

I just stared at Shredder.

"I know you've been hurt by this and for that I'm sorry, but having Kensington go after Luke in a controlled situation was our best bet at nailing him."

I lowered my eyes and looked at my hands, which where clasped in my lap. "Why did you have to lie to me? Why did you have to send me off on a fool's errand? You should have trusted me. I could have helped."

Shredder once again put a finger under my chin and lifted my eyes to meet his. "You're an amazing woman. You're strong and caring, intelligent and athletic. But you don't know how to follow orders. You're a loose cannon who rolls around changing direction at will. You're impulsive and spontaneous and, as far as the FBI was concerned, a liability. They wanted to detain you while we ran the sting. It was Jason who came up with the idea of keeping you busy instead."

"So sending Komo to Maui was my brother's idea?"

"Yes, but the surfing competition was mine, though it wasn't planned. I could see you weren't going to leave things alone and I couldn't have you following me or Kensington around, so I improvised. Actually you improvised. I just had to stand there while you went off on one of your tangents and came up with the prefect plan."

"And you made sure I got a spot in the competition?"

Shredder nodded.

That explained how I got in when there were qualifiers who clearly were better than me. Shredder had figured I'd be busy at the competition during the time the sting was set to go down. And I would have, if Dad hadn't run into Komo and my mom hadn't mentioned it to me.

"Look, I know you're mad at all of us and I can understand that," Shredder continued, "but you shouldn't be mad at Luke. He was against lying to you from the moment he became involved. It wasn't until I threatened to detain you if he didn't cooperate that he agreed to our plan. He loves you. He'd never intentionally hurt you."

I didn't respond, but I did think about what he'd said. I hadn't told Luke about the fake smuggling ring when Shredder told me not to, and I hadn't had half as good a reason to keep my secret from him as he'd had to keep his from me.

"I should go to him."

"Yes." Shredder smiled. "I think you should."

I hugged him and then headed into the condo to get my keys. I tossed a couple of things into a bag and then got in my Jeep.

The drive between the complex and Luke's ranch was both too long and too short. While I couldn't wait to make things right between us, I had no idea what I was going to say to him to do it. I'd told him that I never wanted to see him again. The fact that he hadn't followed me was proof he'd taken me at my word.

I know I'm sensitive about people not treating me as a capable adult who can take care of herself. You can say it's one of my hot buttons. It doesn't help that not only am I petite but also the only girl and the youngest child in my family. My dad and brothers have treated me like a fragile flower since the day I was born. I know they think they're looking out for me, but what they're really doing is diminishing me. I don't want to be protected. I don't need to be protected. What I need is for the people who claim to love me to treat me as an equal.

I pulled onto the ranch road and slowly approached the house. This wasn't going to be an easy conversation and I wasn't looking forward to it. I mean really, what could I say that would make things better? What would Luke say?

When I came to the end of the drive, I parked and slowly got out of my Jeep. I climbed the front steps, rang the bell, and then knocked on the door for good measure. In the several seconds it took Luke to answer my heart beat faster than it ever had before. Sure I'd been hurt, but I really didn't want to lose the only man I had ever loved.

I stood perfectly still when Luke opened the door. He started to take a step toward me, then paused. I struggled to find the words necessary to apologize, but all I could come up with were tears. Luke opened his arms and I walked into them.

"I'm so sorry," he whispered against my hair. I buried my face into his chest and he tightened his arms around me. I found I still couldn't speak, so I pulled back slightly, stood on tiptoe, and kissed him gently on the mouth.

Chapter 13

Saturday, April 1

Luke and I stood across from each other with the minister between us. I wore a yellow dress that matched the flowers I held and he wore a white dress shirt with black pants and a black tie that made him look like a dashing James Bond. My heart pounded as the music began and all eyes turned to the end of the lawn, where Janice stood waiting to make the long walk toward the man she would marry. I'm not sure how they managed it, but somehow Tammy Rhea and Emmy Jean had talked Janice and RJ into a big wedding with all the trimmings. Janice and RJ had asked Luke and me to serve as best man and maid of honor because neither had family on the island.

I looked Luke in the eye as Janice and RJ recited the vows they'd written. I couldn't help but wonder if one day it would be Luke and me professing our love for each other in front of our family and friends. Our relationship was still evolving, but I hoped deep in my heart that we would weather the bumps until we found our own happily ever after.

I glanced at my mom and dad, who sat with Tommy between them in the second row. It turned out Dad and RJ were old friends, something I hadn't been aware of until I'd seen my parents' names on the guest list. All three looked happy, although they still hadn't found out who Tommy was or where he had come from. He'd told my parents he didn't remember ever having a mother. He mentioned a man who used to take care of him named Roger Pitman who he assumed was his father, but he didn't know that for certain. Roger was homeless and liked to move around, so Tommy had never lived in a real house or gone to school. Tommy said Roger had disappeared a year or so ago, which was when Buck had started watching out for him. Buck also wandered off for days at a time, so Tommy ended up mostly looking out for himself.

Tommy's fingerprints weren't on file and the woman from Child Protective Services hadn't been able to track down any information on either a Roger or a Tommy Pitman. There were no missing persons reports indicating anyone was looking for Tommy, so my parents had been made temporary foster parents while those in charge tried to sort everything out.

I smiled at Luke as the minster declared Janice and RJ man and wife. He smiled back and I knew that despite everything that had happened we were going to be okay. Vince Kensington had been arrested and an official investigation had been opened to determine whether he was responsible for not only Blaze Whitmore's death but the deaths of the three other men he'd been investigating as well. Jason and I had chatted, and even though I was still pretty peeved, I'd decided to forgive him. He was, after all, my brother. I'd wanted to stay mad at Shredder, but he was so dang charming when he wanted to be that it was nearly impossible. He still hadn't told me exactly who he'd worked for, but I supposed there were some secrets that needed to be kept even from curious people like me.

Luke and I followed Janice and RJ back down the grassy aisle that had been created by the rented folding chairs. It was a beautiful day with sunny skies and temps in the seventies, which was perfect for the party the Southern sisters had organized.

"That was really nice," I whispered to Luke.

"It wasn't as spectacular as a horseback wedding, but yes, it was nice."

I rolled my eyes. I honestly couldn't tell if Luke was just teasing me of if he was serious, but there was no way I was getting married on the back of a giant fleabag who had the potential to stomp me to death. I glanced toward the pasture where several horses, including Lucifer, were grazing. Despite my general dislike of horses, I was more than a little relieved that Luke's vet had isolated the bug causing Lucifer's illness and the black beauty was going to be all right.

"I was thinking that maybe the two of us should take a trip this summer," Luke commented. "If you can get the time off, that is."

"I have vacation time coming to me, although spring is a slower time at the resort, so maybe that would be better. What did you have in mind?"

"I'm thinking a little cabin on the lake. Just the two of us with no family or jobs or murder investigations to distract us from focusing on each other."

"Do you have a particular cabin in mind?"

"Actually I do. I have an uncle who owns a quaint little cabin right on a lake in a charming town called Ashton Falls."

Next from Kathi Daley Books

Head to Ashton Falls with Luke and Lani as they join Zak and Zoe in a murder mystery treasure hunt over spring break.

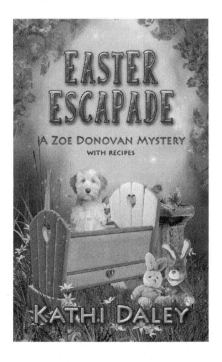

Recipes

Recipes from Kathi

Banana Cheese Pie
Supereasy Hawaiian Pie
Pineapple Upside-down Cake

Recipes from Readers

Margarita Pie—submitted by Jeannie
Daniel
Aggression Cookies—submitted by Joanne
Kocourek
Vanilla Cream Pie—submitted by Connie
Correll
Pecan Turtle Candy—submitted by Vivian
Shane

Banana Cheese Pie

2 large bananas
1 ready-made graham cracker crust (or make your own)
8 oz. cream cheese, softened
1 large box vanilla instant pudding
3 cups milk
1 small container Cool Whip
1 cup macadamia nuts, chopped

Slice bananas into pie crust. Mix cream cheese, pudding, and milk together and let set for 5 minutes. Pour over bananas in piecrust. Spread Cool Whip on top and garnish with macadamia nuts.

Supereasy Hawaiian Pie

1 can crushed pineapple, undrained (20 oz.)
1 box instant vanilla pudding mix (6 servings)
8 oz. sour cream
1 9-in. graham cracker crust
1 small container Cool Whip
I can sliced pineapple
8 maraschino cherries
½ cup flaked coconut

In a large bowl, combine crushed pineapple with its syrup, dry pudding mix, and sour cream. Mix until well combined. Spoon into pie crust. Frost with Cool Whip and decorate top with pineapple slices and cherries. Sprinkle with coconut.

Cover and chill at least 2 hours before serving.

Easy Pineapple Upside-Down Cake

¼ cup butter or margarine
1 cup brown sugar, packed
1 can (20 oz.) pineapple slices in juice, drained, juice reserved
1 jar (6 oz.) maraschino cherries without stems, drained
1 box yellow cake mix, eggs, and oil called for on box

Heat oven to 350 degrees. In 9 x 13-inch pan, melt butter in oven. Sprinkle brown sugar evenly over butter. Arrange pineapple slices on brown sugar. Place cherry in center of each pineapple slice and arrange remaining cherries around slices; press gently into brown sugar.

Add enough water to reserved pineapple juice to match liquid called for on cake mix box. Make batter as directed on box, substituting pineapple juice mixture for the water. Pour batter over pineapple and cherries.

Bake 42 to 48 minutes (44 to 53 minutes for dark or nonstick pan) or until toothpick inserted in center comes out clean. Immediately run knife around side of pan to loosen cake. Place heatproof serving plate upside down onto pan; turn plate and pan over. Leave pan over cake 5 minutes so brown-sugar topping can drizzle over cake; remove pan. Cool 30 minutes. Serve warm or cool. Store covered in refrigerator.

Margarita Pie

Submitted by Jeannie Daniel

1 tbs. unflavored gelatin
½ cup lime juice
½ cup tequila
½ cup sugar
¼ tsp. salt
4 egg yolks, lightly beaten
2 tsp. grated lime peel
3 tbs. orange-flavored liqueur
1 9-in. prebaked pie shell

Dissolve gelatin in a little of the lime juice in a saucepan. Add the tequila, the remaining lime juice, sugar, and salt and cook over low heat until the gelatin is dissolved completely. Add the egg yolks and continue cooking until mixture starts to thicken. Remove from heat and stir in the lime peel and orange liqueur. Chill this mixture in fridge for a half hour or so. Spoon into baked pie shell and top with whipped cream. Return to the fridge and chill for an hour or until good and firm.

Aggression Cookies

Submitted by Joanne Kocourek

An allergy-friendly oatmeal recipe (eliminate nuts and chocolate chips if allergic).

Sometimes we get mad, and sometimes kids get mad, and that's okay. The problem comes when kids can't figure out how to channel their anger, but this cookie recipe can fix that. So, if you have mad kids, make aggression cookies! I don't know where this recipe originated. My grandmother made them with my brother and me.

6 cups old-fashioned oatmeal (not quick oats)
3 cups brown sugar
1 tbs. baking soda
3 cups flour
3 cups butter
2 cups chopped nuts (optional)
1½ cups chocolate chips (white, milk, or

semisweet) (optional)
Granulated sugar for flattening cookies

With a spoon, mix all your dry ingredients together in a gigantic bowl (the largest one you have might not be big enough).

With your hands (ha ha! Here's where the aggression comes in!) mix all your butter in with your dry ingredients. This may take quite a bit of time as you mush it all together, or just think of it as a minimanicure of butter/oatmeal for your hands. Keep going until the whole mixture is as mixed as it can get. It'll be a little dryer than regular cookie dough, but kids can eat it without being sickened by the eggs...because there aren't any!

Place spoonful-sized balls 2 inches apart on a baking sheet.

Butter the bottom of a small glass, dip it into granulated sugar, and mash the balls flat. You may need to rebutter the glass a few times during the process, but redip in sugar for each ball, otherwise the dough will stick to the glass (or flatten cookies with a fork).

Bake at 330 degrees for 9 to 12 minutes.

Let cookies cool completely before handling.

Note: If you aren't feeling aggressive, or if you just want to be a party pooper, you can use a mixer, but we won't guarantee the results.

Vanilla Cream Pie

Submitted by Connie Correll

Mix in medium saucepan ⅔ cup sugar, ½ tsp. salt, 2½ tbs. cornstarch, 1 tbs. flour. Gradually add 3 cups milk.

Cook over moderate heat, stirring constantly, until mixture thickens and boils. Boil 1 minute. Remove from heat and stir in 3 egg yolks, slightly beaten.

Return mixture to heat. Boil 1 minute more, stirring constantly. Remove from heat and blend in 1 tbs. real butter and 1½ tsp. vanilla.

While cooling, stir occasionally, before pouring into graham cracker crust.

Add sliced bananas or coconut to pie shell and cover with mixture and real whipped cream. For added fun try these variations: chocolate cream pie (follow the above recipe except increase sugar to 1½ cups sugar and 3 oz. chocolate) and almond cream pie (follow the above recipe except in place of vanilla use ½ tsp. almond extract and add ½ cup slivered almonds).

A side note to this story: The first banana cream pie I ever made was for my husband eighteen years ago, after his last radiation treatment. That week alone he and our six-year-old son devoured three pies between them.

Pecan Turtle Candy

Submitted by Vivian Shane

I remember making these with my mom when I was young...and now I make them with my grandkids.

2 cups pecan halves
36 unwrapped caramels
36 chocolate Kisses

Arrange 5 pecan halves to a cookie sheet to resemble a turtle head and legs. Place a caramel in the center, making 36 turtles. Bake in 325-degree oven for about 5 minutes. Remove from oven and flatten caramels over pecans with a buttered spatula. Place a chocolate Kiss on the top of the caramel. Once the chocolate softens from the warm caramel, spread it around the top.

Books by Kathi Daley

Come for the murder, stay
for the romance.

Zoe Donovan Cozy Mystery:

Halloween Hijinks
The Trouble With Turkeys
Christmas Crazy
Cupid's Curse
Big Bunny Bump-off
Beach Blanket Barbie
Maui Madness
Derby Divas
Haunted Hamlet
Turkeys, Tuxes, and Tabbies
Christmas Cozy
Alaskan Alliance
Matrimony Meltdown
Soul Surrender
Heavenly Honeymoon
Hopscotch Homicide
Ghostly Graveyard
Santa Sleuth
Shamrock Shenanigans
Kitten Kaboodle
Costume Catastrophe
Candy Cane Caper

Holiday Hangover
Easter Escapade – *April 2017*

Zimmerman Academy The New Normal
Ashton Falls Cozy Cookbook

Tj Jensen Paradise Lake Mysteries by Henery Press

Pumpkins in Paradise
Snowmen in Paradise
Bikinis in Paradise
Christmas in Paradise
Puppies in Paradise
Halloween in Paradise
Treasure in Paradise – *April 2017*
Fireworks in Paradise – *October 2017*

Seacliff High Mystery:

The Secret
The Curse
The Relic
The Conspiracy
The Grudge

Whales and Tails Cozy Mystery:

Romeow and Juliet
The Mad Catter
Grimm's Furry Tail
Much Ado About Felines
Legend of Tabby Hollow
Cat of Christmas Past
A Tale of Two Tabbies
The Great Catsby
Count Catula
The Cat of Christmas Present
A Winter's Tail
The Taming of the Tabby – *June 2017*

Sand and Sea Hawaiian Mystery:

Murder at Dolphin Bay
Murder at Sunrise Beach
Murder at the Witching Hour
Murder at Christmas
Murder at Turtle Cove
Murder at Water's Edge – *May 2017*

Road to Christmas Romance:

Road to Christmas Past

Writer's Retreat Southern Mystery:

First Case – *May 2017*
Second Look – *July 2017*

Kathi Daley lives with her husband, kids, grandkids, and Bernese mountain dogs in beautiful Lake Tahoe. When she isn't writing, she likes to read (preferably at the beach or by the fire), cook (preferably something with chocolate or cheese), and garden (planting and planning, not weeding). She also enjoys spending time on the water when she's not hiking, biking, or snowshoeing the miles of desolate trails surrounding her home.

Kathi uses the mountain setting in which she lives, along with the animals (wild and domestic) that share her home, as inspiration for her cozy mysteries.

Kathi is a top 100 mystery writer for Amazon and won the 2014 award for both Best Cozy Mystery Author and Best Cozy Mystery Series.

She currently writes five series: Zoe Donovan Cozy Mysteries, Whales and Tails Island Mysteries, Sand and Sea Hawaiian Mysteries, Tj Jensen Paradise Lake Mysteries, and Seacliff High Teen Mysteries.

Giveaway:

I do a giveaway for books, swag, and gift cards every week in my newsletter, *The Daley Weekly*
http://eepurl.com/NRPDf

Other links to check out:
Kathi Daley Blog – publishes each Friday
http://kathidaleyblog.com
Webpage – **www.kathidaley.com**
Facebook at Kathi Daley Books –
www.facebook.com/kathidaleybooks
Kathi Daley Teen –
www.facebook.com/kathidaleyteen
Kathi Daley Books Group Page –
https://www.facebook.com/groups/569578823146850/
E-mail – **kathidaley@kathidaley.com**
Goodreads –
https://www.goodreads.com/author/show/7278377.Kathi_Daley
Twitter at Kathi Daley@kathidaley –
https://twitter.com/kathidaley
Amazon Author Page –
https://www.amazon.com/author/kathidaley

BookBub –
**https://www.bookbub.com/authors/
kathi-daley**

Pinterest –
**http://www.pinterest.com/kathidale
y/**

Made in the USA
San Bernardino, CA
23 August 2018